FITZPATRICK

DEMON
MATT TIDE

DEMON
TIDE

Matt Fitzpatrick

Woodhall Press
Norkwall, CT

woodhall press

Woodhall Press, 81 Old Saugatuck Road, Norwalk, CT 06855
WoodhallPress.com

Cover design: Asha Hossain
Layout artist: Christina Cagliotti-Diglio

Library of Congress Cataloging-in-Publication Data available
ISBN 978-1-949116-58-8 (paper: alk paper)
ISBN 978-1-949116-59-5 (electronic)

First Edition
Distributed by Independent Publishers Group
(800) 888-4741
Printed in the United States of America

This is a work of fiction. Names, characters, business, events and incidents are the products of the author's imagination. Any resemblance to actual persons, living or dead, or actual events is purely coincidental.

In memory of Tori, and all singers of sweet, silent serenades

"They sift the human storm for souls, eat flesh of reason, fill tombs with sinners. They frenzy forth. . . . Such are the autumn people."

—**Ray Bradbury**

The great fish moved silently through the night water . . .

—**Peter Benchley**

Fall 2018: Excerpt of the U.S. Government press conference announcing the formal approval of Tsulio

The corpulent spokesman took the podium.

The crisis of opioid addiction is an issue of great concern for our nation. Addressing it is a public health priority for the FDA and other agencies. They are now taking new steps to more actively confront this crisis, while also paying careful attention to the needs of patients and physicians managing pain. As part of these considerations, there's been an important and robust public debate leading up to the regulatory decision on Tsoulio that merits a response. We want to take this opportunity to address some of the concerns that were raised, and, more broadly, how we believe the Government should consider the approval of new opioid pain medications that can help fill targeted medical needs.

Looking beyond this particular drug approval, we believe that we should be doing more to evaluate each novel candidate opioid, not just as an independent review decision, but rather in the context of the overall therapeutic armamentarium that's available to patients and providers. As we look at the public health implications of each new approval, we should evaluate whether we need to take additional steps to systematically review new opioids relative to the comparative benefits and risks of others already on the market. We will be doing more to ensure that new opioids are sufficiently better than existing drugs to justify their addition to the market in the context of the current crisis of abuse . . .

CHAPTER ONE

250 miles East of Cape Ann, Massachusetts, Summer 2019

The late-spring marauder marched across the ocean delivering sustained winds of forty knots with intermittent gusts that bitched over sixty. It was born at forty-five degrees on the ship's compass and punished all obstacles like a prison escapee.

The seventy-two-foot commercial fishing vessel bore a stark resemblance to the boat made famous by Sebastian Junger's *Perfect Storm* two decades earlier. While its intimidating presence commanded respect at the dock, with its massive steel hull and surly crew, at the moment it was a rubber duck in a tub. The captain and crew were trying to maintain station in the wheelhouse, as the relentless pounding had no end. Minutes spit out hours.

Walls of water twenty to thirty feet high bombarded the vessel's port side as she lumbered, southbound, trying to jettison the storm's clutches. Captain Ornellas kept a firm grip on the wheel as he attempted to bark out commands, which only fell on deaf ears as the shrieks of the wind controlled all volume.

Ornellas looked around the station and took inventory of his suffering crew. Some wore white mask-like faces from a bad zombie movie, with empty, sunken eyes and long, gaping mouths. Others quietly vomited in corners behind shorted-out electronics. With a quick count, the captain realized a skipper's greatest fear. He was one crewman shy.

"Where's Selkirk? Hey! *Where is Selkirk!*" shrieked Ornellas, whose words only evoked more shrieks from the gale's nor'easterly screams.

Ornellas looked over at First Mate Bramberg, whose eyes were spinning like a slot machine.

"Bram! Where the hell is Selkirk?"

With a quick head jerk, Bramberg processed the captain's question and answered with a chest heave that blasted up a fountain of yellow bile, followed by a few tablespoons of maroon to cap off the retch.

"Shit!" said the captain, shaking his head in frustration.

By instinct, he grabbed the radio's microphone and was about to speak, then burst into a madman's laughter at the futility of the action.

Suddenly, a sneaky defensive-lineman rogue wave busted through the highest rollers.

Smash! All of the helm station's portside windows erupted in a cascade of flying glass.

Ornellas screamed, "Get the plywood! Get the hammer and plywood!"

There was no response from the other crewmen in the wheelhouse. The only sound that could be heard was Bramberg's dry heaves.

Meanwhile, belowdecks, Simon Selkirk was anticipating that floating, peaceful dance partner who would caress his hand once he tasted the sweet poison. He had snagged this assignment during a last-minute callout offer over a couple of beers at Kelsey's, after a long, lousy-paying week at his day job. Normally, Selkirk could be found pouring cement forms for the new population of yuppies moving into Guild Harbor and planting the seeds of McMansions and gentrification.

Most locals were steadfast in their desire to not fall prey to the world of window boxes and community theater now ruling their northern, once-hearty, bare-knuckle fishing town of Newburyport. They liked Guild Harbor the way it had been for over three hundred and fifty years, yet the newcomers arrived with the oldest enticement in the world. Cash, with a running tab that knew no governance.

At first, spending a couple of weeks at sea with Captain Ornellas had seemed like it would be a welcome vacation for Selkirk. A way to roll up his sleeves and celebrate his heritage. The trip's plans had come together quickly, and he knew and trusted the roster of guys who had already signed on.

What he had not looked forward to were the inevitable withdrawal symptoms from the needle's recent marks, which would occur during the first day out. He hadn't anticipated how difficult it would be to score a fix with the North Atlantic's temper in full rage.

Suddenly, Selkirk felt a floating weightlessness as he was picked up by the starboard side of the bilge and smashed against a white-hot exhaust manifold. For a split second, the searing heat burned through his foul-weather suit, yet he did not feel the pain nor smell the burning neoprene.

With his wrist already sprained from getting tossed against an ice locker, he felt around his jacket for the syringe, already loaded. Fortunately it had not yet discharged.

Another bull wave's crest took out the remaining antennae on the wheelhouse as the wind quickly shifted another ten degrees to the east. The underside of the massive roll brought a split second of calm until the following wall of water smash-mouthed dead center to the port side. That blast sent Selkirk crashing against an exhaust pipe. As the ship pivoted to stay upright, he slid headfirst into a fish storage container whose door had been blown clean off seconds before.

Selkirk took a quick physical inventory and felt ten fingers and toes. He rubbed the left side of his body against a mound of ice while checking on the status of the syringe in his right pocket. He exhaled gratitude. It felt intact. While getting tossed around he used any part of his body available to serve as a barrier between his needle and that which meant to cause harm. He was a frantic mother cradling her baby while running out of a fire, sidestepping the flames.

There was a momentary lapse in the storm's fury as Selkirk sat up against the pile of ice. His shaking had gotten so bad, he had serious doubts whether he could extract the syringe without squandering its contents.

With his right hand, he tore at the rubber on his left arm, knowing that he could never roll up his gear far enough to hit the usual vein.

Instead, he ripped off his left glove and stretched out his fingers, only to see that they were on the verge of frostbite. For a moment, the multicolored blood vessels made him think of the side of a childhood ice-cream truck whose bell screamed through the neighborhood with a dozen children chasing behind. It wasn't the actual ice cream that stirred euphoria—it was those few moments when you were called up to the portable counter and got to select a cold treat. It was the moment of *choosing* that felt exciting.

As Selkirk looked at his hands, he was trying to find a fresh place between his fingers when *BLAST!* A wave hit the port stern and ripped a fire extinguisher off the wall, causing the unit to tumble while spewing white foam.

Upon looking at the blown-out webs of his fingers, he had to change his course of action. Most of the veins in his arm were flat tires. He was shaking badly and started to dream about dragons. A young boy being chased by beasts through the forest, toward the warmth and safety of a castle.

SMASH!

Another wave hit, yet the bilge area experienced little effect.

Selkirk realized he had no saliva left and was having trouble breathing. Yet, he yearned for the nectar.

With his sprained right hand, he pulled the syringe out of his right pocket. It was locked and loaded, pleading to Selkirk to unleash its shackles.

After giving up all hope of finding any bodily avenues in his left hand or fingers, he opted for the path of least resistance.

He slipped off his work-strap plastic eyeglasses and tossed them into a pool of melting ice. He held the syringe before his face, checking to make sure it would be a sufficient delivery. With his left hand he placed his thumb at the base, which proved almost impossible. The shakes knocked his grip three inches to either side every two seconds.

Selkirk held the syringe high and plunged it into his right eyeball. He didn't really care, but he hoped he would only pierce the white of his eye. He heard a slight *pop*, like the sound of gelled pudding being pierced. He met his target and pushed the plunger with his thumb.

As if Mother Nature had bestowed a gift, suddenly the storm ceased. The waves were still.

He expected to have trouble seeing due to his choice of entry, yet he had never experienced such visual clarity until that moment.

The ocean was a Vermont pond.

All was still and quiet, with a new sun's rays high-beaming through the porthole.

He marveled at how peaceful everything was, and how the swans barely made a wake as they swam by. A butterfly nestled down on a leaf next to his right cheek. The insect spread its wings, puffed out its thin chest, and then bowed its head to welcome sleep.

CHAPTER TWO

Dunlap Neck, Guild Harbor, Massachusetts

"He what?! What happened to this kid?"

Captain Jib Scola paced the well-worn mahogany floor of his harborfront home office on Dunlap Neck, his phone to his ear. It was one of the finest areas in Guild Harbor, Massachusetts, and not a likely location for those who had known Jib since childhood.

The captain was a certified townie in the history-rich, small New England coastal city. Like most of his peers, he had grown up hard in a hard town. His father and grandfather were not only part of Guild Harbor's storied fishing community, but they both gave their lives to the sea on every level. Each perished in horrific North Atlantic storms while plying their trade, but neither was missed that much by the families they left behind. They were rarely home, and when they were, alcohol assumed command of their bodies and minds. They cast neither physical presence nor emotional shadows.

"Yeah, Jib," responded Eel Korvitz, Jib's lifelong friend and first mate, as well as his right-hand man in their latest business venture, which afforded Jib an envious existence on the Neck.

"They found him curled up on his back like a crab flipped by a wave. He was in a crawlspace down in an ice storage area, dead as gull shit. At first they figured maybe he'd slipped and smacked his head during the storm, but the Essex County medical examiner doesn't buy it. They say he blanked out on smack, which didn't take a coroner to determine. Damn needle was next to him in the bilge. They say he stuck the thing in his eye!"

"My God" was all Jib could mutter.

Eel continued. "Anyway, the boat finally made it home after the storm took a powder. They found the kid's body already on ice, so they didn't have to move 'im too fast."

Jib was quiet on the other end as Eel went on with fervor. "I mean, these young guys are overdoing it on the shit! Maybe we oughta put on the package like, I dunno, a warning label or something? You know? Ever hear of *caveat emptor?*"

"Yes, Eel, it was stamped on my marriage license," responded Scola.

Eel grunted, "I dunno, Jib. You can make light, but we really need to think things over. Too many people sense what we're up to. It doesn't help that all anyone has ever seen you do is chase cod and haddock, and now you hold court out there in your seaside palace. It's getting way too obvious, and we're gonna be exposed. I dunno, man. You're wearing the spoils, Skippah."

Jib couldn't afford to have his partner doubting their efforts right now.

Korvitz kept going. "What happened to *Hey Eel, we'll just make a couple of runs, that's all. Just a few smash and grabs. Y'know? Get us through the winter?* What happened to that mission?"

Jib tried to defuse the tension. "Yeah, yeah, I know we started out modest. But Eel, it's been six years, and things change. I didn't foresee how much fruit would spill outta the bush."

"That's right, six years. And how many of our customers are dead?" Eel coughed and continued. "Jib, I'm as guilty as you in all this. I loved the money for a while, but now I'm getting nervous. People talk in this town. Shit, people talk in every New England town, but there are more rumors around here than clamshells. We had a good thing going, man, but now you've gone all Hollywood! Buying a big house, fancy cars, dinners, broads . . . You've become our town's version of Puff Daddy. Dammit, Jib, don't you think people notice?"

Jib dismissively grunted. "People talk because they're envious."

"Okay, Skip. But, they won't be so jealous when you and I are wearing sundresses down in a cellblock at Cedar Junction."

Jib paused and picked up a pile of mail that his maid, Amina, had left on the edge of his desk. In a business that was growing more complicated by the day, at least he had Amina to come home to. While the two were not lovers, she did provide his home with a much-needed peaceful air.

He flipped through the various letters, deep in thought as he tried to compose a response to his partner. One hot pink envelope stuck out amid a sea of white and gray. He started to rip it open on one end.

"Just relax, Eel. Let's wait and get all the facts about what happened to that kid on the sword boat. I'll go down tomorrow and talk to . . . What the fuck . . ."

Jib noticed that the envelope had suddenly become lighter.

He looked down and realized that its contents had fallen out into a small, white powdery mound on his oaken desk.

He removed the card and whispered aloud the words *Get well soon.*

CHAPTER THREE

Mary Ann Scola, Boston College

Mary Ann Scola was exhausted from last night's festivities. She freed the bottle of Bacardi from her nightstand drawer and took a knock to trim the sails.

"Dammit," she said to herself. "Why did he have to be such an asshole?"

She got up and quietly turned to her closet so as not to wake her roommate, who was curled up next to some carpenter ant from Randolph.

"Nice," she muttered.

With books and pens thrown in her backpack, she carefully exited and locked her dorm room in Gonzaga Hall on BC's upper campus. She headed down the hallway and passed by some of her dorm mates.

"Hey, Mary Ann!" one of her neighbors called out. "Where are you going in such a hurry? Word is that some senior is gonna bring over a barrel later on. You up for a coupla *bingahs* beforehand?"

Mary Ann paused, to be thoughtful.

"No, thank you, Kathy. My dad e-mailed me that I need to check my snail-mail box."

Kathy replied, "Hey! You might be getting a windfall check!"

Mary Ann politely put her hand up. "No, I doubt it. Most likely it's just a nautical chart highlighted with cod honey holes."

Her floor mate shook her head. "I can't believe you're actually into *fishing.* Yuck."

Mary Ann smirked. "Well, you're not from Guild Harbor."

CHAPTER FOUR

Folly Cove, Cape Ann

Simona's tension-plagued body welcomed gravity, sinking into the ground as her bare feet touched the sand. This was her first day off in over two months, and dammit, she was going to savor it. It was a perfect mid-June day on the North Shore, with warm sun, low humidity, and just enough of an easterly breeze to shoo away the gnats.

She chose her destination carefully. It was not a popular spot for beachgoers, frequented more often by scuba enthusiasts who enjoyed the steep drop-off and the abundance of marine life. The cove was a haven to stripers, lobsters, flounder, and the occasional wandering blue shark.

She selected a spot not too close to the water. She didn't want to have to move with the incoming tide, as she hoped that much of her stay would be comprised of a long-overdue nap. For her pleasure and relaxation, she'd brought along the usual beach bag packed with lotion and a towel, along with a copy of Linda Greenlaw's *Seaworthy*, which she'd been looking forward to reading for years. A chilled bottle of Mezzacorona Pinot Grigio completed her cargo.

She built her encampment, sat back, and poured a healthy serving of wine into the large blue cup. She slowly sipped the Pinot, pursed her glazed lips, and rubbed her long neck.

She wasn't going to think about the gift shop today. Today, it was about her.

Simona and her former college roommate owned a trinket shop roughly thirty minutes away in Salem's Pickering Wharf. Summer was a time for tourist traffic, tourist dollars, and tourist headaches. She was grateful that the business afforded them both a comfortable living, while they laughed and took pride in the fact that they moved dozens of pieces of inventory per day of items that nobody needed. From R-rated tarot cards to aphrodisiac-scented candles, they sold it all as the wallets arrived on buses from across New England looking for souvenirs from the world-renowned Witch City.

As she began to relax, she noticed a couple of divers who had lugged their tanks and gear roughly a quarter of a mile from one of the rare parking spots near the cove. She admired the taller one's tight wet suit, and while Simona had officially reserved this day to be her own time-out for relaxation, at the moment her thoughts turned to images of a roll in the sand.

After a few minutes of letting the wine massage her mind, she mustered up the courage to approach the handsome diver. She figured she'd innocently walk over and ask him to find her a pretty shell while he was spearing for flounder.

She got up and wrapped herself in a multi-flowered sarong and started the hundred-foot trek. As she got closer to the stranger, she noticed that his hard facial features accented the ripe package. Unlike her normal coy self, today was all about her, and dammit, she was going to get noticed.

Three seconds later, she did just that.

"*Eeeek!* Holy shit!" Simona threw her hands in the air in a wild spasm, spilling her wine and jabbing her toes into the ground as if dancing on hot coals.

Immediately, the two divers looked over, dropped their fins and masks, and ran to assist the young woman who looked like she was getting attacked by fire ants.

"Hey, you okay?" asked Simona's would-be suitor.

"N-no! *Look!*" she screamed in reply.

The two divers looked down at the clump of seaweed that seemed to be ruining the woman's day. At first glance, it was just a batch of Atlantic kelp that washes up on every New England beach.

However, this clump had a particularly unique shape and smell.

One of the divers grabbed a stick and began to poke around, only to unveil its underlying contents.

The remains of a wide-smiling, crab-eaten human face.

The divers noticed a pair of hermit crabs crawling out of the one remaining cheek pocket, presumably perturbed at the rumpus that had interrupted their nibbling.

Before they crawled away, the larger one snatched a piece from the crusty lower lip, grabbing a snack to go.

CHAPTER FIVE

Guild Harbor Waterfront

Casino's cell phone began to glow, and he took comfort that the text message had arrived on time. While it was new for him to have to work with an intermediary and not Scola himself, he was not concerned. He'd worked for Jib as a distributor for three years, and Jib's operations always ran smoothly and efficiently.

If the importer now required mules to get the product in the hands of the street dealers, Casino didn't mind. It was smart and good business. And Casino knew that Jib was smart.

With the text having been received, Casino walked around the corner to an alley next to an old fish-processing plant. While the facility had been closed for over ten years, Casino swore he could still smell the putrid fish oil. He looked at his phone and saw that it displayed 1:59 a.m.

He waited patiently and fired up a Marlboro. As he took his first drag, he toe-tapped to some *White Stripes* infectious bass groove that he'd heard on Sirius on the ride over.

His cell now read 2:00 a.m.

Suddenly, he heard the crunch of feet coming from about thirty yards at the far end of the alley. The courier looked rather small to Casino, but the important part was the dark-colored knapsack the mule was carrying. The street dealer knew that the amount promised on the phone would keep him profitable and busy for over a month, even in an area like the North Shore during summer, when demand was high.

The dark figure walked up to Casino without saying a word.

The silence was a little unnerving, and Casino felt the need to break the ice.

"Nice night we're having. Not too humid."

The figure unzipped the sack in continued silence, reached in to retrieve the package, and handed it to Casino. With an open hand the courier then pointed to the wrapped bundle as if to ask the dealer to inspect the contents.

"Oh, sure," Casino said.

He thought this whole exchange was a little creepy and melodramatic, but maybe the mule was just being careful. He noticed that the courier had on leather gloves that seemed unusually small.

Casino opened the end of the package slightly with a nail file.

"Hey buddy, I would never doubt Jib's product, but this whole cloak-and-dagger intermediary thing is new. I'm just gonna dab this and have a little taste."

Casino put the cigarette in his left hand and licked his right index finger. "No" was all the dealer could mutter.

The courier was small, but quick. With the flick of a stiletto blade snatched from the confines of a loose, leather belt, the mule grabbed the back of Casino's long black hair and pulled hard, exposing his neck to the moon's spotlight. Before Casino even realized what was happening, the courier slid the blade across his neck, pausing only for an instant as the knife got caught on a bit of cartilage in the middle of his throat.

Grabbing at his neck, Casino fell to his knees and then to the left, on top of the parcel of spurious heroin.

CHAPTER SIX

Mary Ann Scola, Boston College Mailroom

Mary Ann,

As my daughter, I wish for you nothing but happiness, so I hope that your first year is going well. Imagine, a Scola in college! You're the first in the family, honey!

I've sent you a framed set of lyrics. I hope that you love them, as I love you. It's a song called "Let the Day Begin" by The Call. I hope that these words will bring inspiration.

The fishing has been tough out there. Light catches and heavy weather. But it will turn, honey. Nothing to do with you—just focus on your studies.

I need to ask something of you. Are you still being mentored by that chemistry doctoral student? I was wondering if you could have her call me. I might have a research project for her if she's interested in a little side work, and of course, some extra spending money. We're trying to understand some of these studies that are coming out regarding the microbes and bacteria that are ending up in the ocean due to pollution. Could end up being a thesis for her?

For now, enjoy the lyrics.

With love,

Dad

CHAPTER SEVEN

Kelsey's Bar, Guild Harbor

As in most old New England towns, the Guild Harbor police force was comprised of ninety-nine percent committed, well-intentioned career officers. However, such institutions often possessed an infected underbelly.

Sergeant Anthony O'Doul was Guild Harbor's version of the one leaky bottle in the case of beer. He was raised in a lower-middle-class, Irish-Italian family whose only local claim to fame was that his uncle, Giuseppe Garibaldi—named after an obscure nineteenth-century Italian war general—had caught the flag to win the Greasy Pole Contest that Guild Harbor boasts every summer during St. Anthony's Festival. The famous festival draws crowds from all over New England for a weekend of celebration and revelry that makes New Year's Eve in Tijuana look like a Vatican novena.

While most of O'Doul's colleagues knew that he was on the take, they looked the other way with the classic Boston attitude of *Whaddyagonnado*. None of his antics were hurting anyone in a violent way. They tolerated his collecting the occasional overdue football bet, or shaking down some two-bit weed peddler. But unbeknownst to his fellow officers, O'Doul's extracurricular activities had ramped up over the past few years due to his partnership with Jib Scola.

If his fellow cops were made aware of the fact that O'Doul was formally entrenched in protecting the most dangerous heroin influx the city had ever seen, he would soon end up fastened to the wet end of an anchor chain.

For the time being, though, he enjoyed the thrill of the covert trade, and moreover, was enjoying more money than the last three generations of O'Douls or Garibaldis combined had ever amassed.

This particular afternoon, O'Doul sat in a booth at Kelsey's Bar one block away from the waterfront. Years ago when he was off-duty he could be found on a stool at the now-famous Crow's Nest, the longtime Guild Harbor mainstay that had been annexed by pesky tourists ever since Junger's bestseller went Hollywood.

At Kelsey's, the little bell—put above the pub's door thirty years ago as a joke to warn fishermen of their wives' unwanted arrival—jingled as Jib entered the establishment. He nodded at the barmaid who was squeezing the day's spillage out of a rag, and approached his partner and consultant, Sergeant Tony O'Doul.

"This seat taken?" asked Jib with a slight chuckle.

"Only if you're sellin' bad news," replied O'Doul.

Jib stuck his index finger halfway in the air toward the bar, where the tender correctly interpreted it as the signal for a Bud bottle at room temperature.

"You still swallowing that swill, Jib?" asked Tony. "Shit, a guy with your money oughta be ordering top-shelf, and a round for everyone else while you're at it. Is that what you sip at night, staring out at the harbor in that big ol' mansion of yours?"

"Yeah, well, old habits die hard. And it's not a mansion," said Jib as he waved a dismissive hand above the table. Jib's tone dropped an octave. "Listen, Tony. Like I told you on the phone. Someone sent me anthrax or some shit in the mail. I could be dying as we speak."

Tony rubbed his chin. "Yeah. Well, Jib, I got news for ya. We're *all* in the process of dying as we speak. As every minute goes by, like gulls over the bay."

"Save it, Plato. I gotta major problem here. Someone mailed me some powder with no return address, and my guess is that if you try and take prints off the envelope, you'll find nothing. Plus, it was one of those peel-and-seal envelopes, so there's no chance of picking up saliva DNA."

Sergeant Tony took a haul from his beer as the bartender brought over Jib's warm Bud.

"Warm as rat piss, just the way you like it, captain."

"Thanks, Madge," said Jib as he traded the bottle for a sawbuck.

"My guess is that you're overreacting, Jib," O'Doul said. "I've handled a half-dozen situations like this over the years, and it usually ends up being some kinda Arm and Hammer baking soda shit, or maybe baby powder. Who knows? Maybe it's a sample of your own product? Ever since that anthrax ruckus in the early 2000s, people been using that approach as a scare tactic. The ol' shot across the bow. They're just trying to spook you."

"That's the friggin' point, Tony. Who the hell would have it out for me? We're quiet with our operation, *Sergeant* O'Doul."

Tony sat back. "All right, all right. Where's the shit now?"

"I flushed it down the toilet."

O'Doul burst out laughing. "There goes our evidence. Okay, that's just as well. I doubt that my geeks in the crime lab would test it without an explanation of where it came from."

"I'll just have to watch out for any flu-like symptoms. Whatever . . . Listen, it probably *is* just a warning. But from whom? Who's on to us, and what do they want?"

O'Doul shook his head. "Hey, man, that's the price of poker. We've enjoyed a nice run in a city that walks and talks like a small town. Word gets out. It's friggin' Guild Harbor, Jib. And now with dead kids on fishing boats, the heat is gonna get turned up a lot more. Speaking of which, when's the next shipment due?"

Jib rolled his eyes. "This week. And I've decided it's going to be the last."

"Whaddya mean, the *last?*" asked the sergeant, suddenly perturbed.

Jib immediately responded, "The last, Tony. I mean it—that's it. I'm out. We're cashing in our chips at the damn window. I got enough stashed away that I won't have to worry until the days of bedsores. Everything's paid off. The house, the boats, the cars—all of it. The reward is just not worth the risk anymore. I've got enough money and have enjoyed enough action to last anyone a lifetime. In fact, I've been thinking about what to do with the next shipment, and with this toxic care package, I think I'd like to sub out the transportation duties to a third party."

Jib's last sentence hung in the air.

After several seconds, Tony motioned toward the bar for another round.

"Okay, Jib, let me understand this. You want to send someone else out there to pick up the shipment. Crazy, but all right. I have an idea. Maybe we should take out a classified ad in the *Guild Harbor Daily Times*, if they still even offer such services. I can see it now in bold print: 'Wanted: Brave seafarer to blast offshore in the middle of the night to take possession of a Canadian shipment of heroin. Said parcel is to be distributed on our streets to your kids and troubled love ones. Irish need not apply.' Yeah, man. Shit, they'll be lining up and down the docks for that gig!" Tony burst out laughing at his own joke.

Jib didn't find it funny.

"No, dink. I know a guy. Well, no, I can't say that. I know *of* a guy who might be able to help us."

"Is he local?" asked O'Doul.

"Nah. He *was* in Boston for a long time, but then he had to skip town and ended up down south somewhere. He wouldn't tell me. We met years ago through a mutual captain friend.

"Anyway, over the years we've stayed in touch. Not often, maybe an e-mail once a year or so. He's a lawyer or some kind of big shot, but he also had a lethal side career that he only shared with a select few, mostly mob guys and dishonest, rogue CEO types."

"Wait a minute," said Tony. "You tellin' me that you're friends with that ghost-assassin who's been knockin' off those high-profile hits in Boston but has never been caught? I thought that was just a media myth to sell papers. C'mon, that's crazy."

"Well, that's what I'm telling you. Even assassins keep in touch. As I said, it's only once a year, at best."

"How much does this guy know about our operation?" said Tony. "And how much do you know about *his*? It seems kinda dangerous to be talkin' about that shit over the Internet where some computer geek in, like, Sri Lanka can hack in and read it."

"Our correspondence is pretty vanilla. We talk boats, fishing, whatever. Shit like that. Let the damn FBI hack into my computer. They ain't findin' squat." Jib took a swig of his beer. "Anyway, I think he can help us. I actually heard from him recently, first time in over a year. He mentioned that he knows a guy who he thought might be heading toward the Boston area, on the run from some drug cartel thing. Obviously, he told this to me in *mariner code*. He described the guy, so I put my feelers out, first in Boston, then, the surrounding area. Long story short, our guy has been laying low right here in Guild Harbor."

"No way, Jib. That's too much of a coincidence."

"Maybe," said Jib. "But coincidences do happen, and they can run in your favor. I'm gonna request a meeting and then we'll know for sure. It turns out that the guy is tucked in at Cape Ann Boat Basin. He's been living here for a coupla months with some kind of lackey or dimwitted first mate. I guess the guy's pretty well known in the low-tide pools in Florida. He's a smuggler or a drug-runner type. Ya know, a real 'treetop flyer,' but in a boat.

"The way he was described to me was that he woulda made a great *Miami Vice* character back in the day. Apparently, he's very good at what he does and rumor has it, that he's tight, clean and thorough. Doesn't drink anymore, no drugs, and just the occasional tramp here and there, but never on an assignment. He's a rare and dying breed of pro."

While O'Doul was curious, he couldn't help chuckling. "What the hell's he doing on Cape Ann? Painting Motif Number One?"

Jib shook his head. "Funny. No, like I said, he got in some jam down south and needed a coastal hideout where he could remain anonymous."

Jib paused as two more beers were placed in the middle of the table.

"Thanks, Madge," said O'Doul. "All right, so what's this guy's name?"

"Captain Shark Bertolami," responded Jib.

"Huh," Tony grunted, cleared his throat. "Guineas don't come cheap. Especially if he's on the lam. For us to find guys who are professional *and* quiet, it ain't easy. This is not exactly South Beach or Havana."

"No, it's not," responded Jib. "However, if we can get this guy to make a run, even if he takes a big bite out of the job, we can still go out on a profitable high note."

"Yeah," said Tony, "how do you figure?"

"The stuff that Eel and I have been bringing in, as you know, gets cut, sliced, and diced a dozen ways. Shit, at the end of the process, the guys on the street are selling product that's *maybe* ten percent pure. Once they add in all the talcum powder and sugar, the junk's almost totally watered down. That's where the fentanyl has been coming into play."

"Great, Jib," said O'Doul. "That's probably what killed the kid on the boat."

"Unfortunately, yes. That's another reason why we need to get out."

Jib took a slug of his Bud and continued. "There's a new drug on the market. It was recently FDA-approved, but it's not available to the public yet. Military-grade stuff, designed to be used on the battlefield. This shit is *ten times* more powerful than fentanyl. Bottom line, we cut our stash with the new stuff and we can multiply our distribution tenfold. We make a crusher of a score, and then we retire. Neat. Tidy. *Au revoir, mon ami.*"

Tony scratched at his two-day stubble.

"What's this new stuff called, and how the hell do we get our hands on it?"

Without hesitation, Jib responded. "It's from one of the drug-testing labs that's still experimenting with the stuff. It's called Tsulio, and our Canadian contacts have access to it from one of their sites. We can only get it once. It's military-grade and government-protected. Once the lab picks up on a missing batch, there will be no second helping."

O'Doul saw where this was going.

"Okay, I get it. We make a huge score, and then you, Eel, and I go our separate ways, never to be seen in this town again. I kinda like it. Been wanting to get back to the Bahamas one of these days. But lemme ask you—are you positive that we can only get to this stuff once?"

"Yes, at least from this particular source. Once our Nurse Ratched from Canada steals the stuff, it's only a matter of time before she gets caught, so she's planning on leaving work that day in Nova Scotia with a suitcase in her trunk. She knows the risks, and the cost. It's either she delivers the goods, makes a score, and goes squirrel, or she's gonna end up rotting in a jail cell, accused of international narcotics trafficking, with a product that both governments are trying to keep on the down-low."

"Damn, Jib. You're talking about a major finale. Kinda sad to see it end, now that all these grandiose ideas are finally percolating. I take it you can approach this Captain Shark fella without a lot of noise?"

"Yeah, tomorrow morning."

"How's Eel reacting to all this?"

"He's one step away from cracking at the seams, but I'm confident he can play it cool for one last operation. Any more than that, though, and we risk him becoming a potential liability. And then the possible outcomes are endless."

Upon uttering those words, Jib Scola realized for the first time that his once-solid clandestine operation now resembled a bayou cabin an hour before Katrina.

CHAPTER EIGHT

Cape Ann Boat Basin, aboard the *Booty Call*

The sun-bronzed figure of Captain Shark Bertolami glistened in the mid-morning light. He was aboard his fishing boat, which for the last year had served as a floating hideout for him and his longtime loyal first mate, Peeler. The two smugglers had been on the run after leaving the Georgia coast following a particularly risky and flawed mission that did not satisfy their temporary employer, the infamous Don Juan Conzalez.

Conzalez had hired the two pirates to retrieve some lost contraband off the Florida coast, and in a mistake on his part, he had sent along his beloved niece as chaperone and protector of the mission's integrity. In an industry teeming with drunks and thieves, Shark could be counted on to execute as instructed, and only resorted to violence when all other options had been exhausted. Despite his clean résumé and professional reputation, the Don felt the need to send Jillian along to oversee the operation. In no way a wallflower, she was well-versed in weaponry, martial arts, and all things security-related in a business that often required such actions.

Shark and Peeler were hiding among fishermen and weekend warrior pleasure boaters a thousand miles north of their home because the Conzalez mission had gone badly awry, ending with Peeler sticking the business end of a fishing gaffe into the bottom of Jillian's spine in the middle of a standoff over the mission's progress.

It started after their first dive down to the site of the sunken contraband. When they came back aboard to freshen their air supply, Peeler realized their friend and business partner, Justin McGee, was running into serious problems on a mission of his own, not too far away.

When Shark realized what was happening, he instructed Peeler to weigh anchor so they could go assist their friends in distress. This made Jillian so irate that she trained a pistol on Shark and instructed him to continue the Don's work. The situation was going to end with the two smugglers jumping back into the water, or the boat heading out to rendezvous with Justin, minus one passenger.

The scene reached an irreversible crescendo when Peeler plunged the fishing gaffe into Jillian's back, both ending her life and losing Shark's coveted mission purse.

By the time the Don had pieced together what had happened, their vessel, *Booty Call*, was blasting full throttle up the southeastern coast with South Carolina to the boat's port side. After ducking into various ports and marinas along the Eastern Seaboard, paying off dockmasters to let them snag a slip that kept the boat out of sight, the two outlaws sought a semipermanent home in a quiet, out-of-the-way marina in Guild Harbor. When they arrived, they were tired and sick of the sound of their own engine. They needed time to rest, regroup, and strategize.

"Hey, Peel," Shark called to his first mate, who was busy splicing anchor line. "You hungry? Let's wrap up these chores by noon and walk over to the Spillway. I could use a big ol' bowl of fish chowder."

"Roger, Skip. Just gimme another ten minutes," said Peeler, who also started to feel hungry at the sound of a lunch break. "Hey, I forgot to mention that I found this on the helm seat when I woke up this morning." Peeler crossed the deck and handed the note to Shark.

The captain was immediately concerned when he saw *Captain Shark Bertolami* typed on the nondescript, light brown envelope. His muscles tightened and his neck grew stiff. Very few people knew his last name.

He stretched his hand over the starboard side and held the envelope up to the sunlight to try and see the outline of its contents. At first glance it appeared to be a single sheet of paper.

"G'won, Skip. Open it. Maybe it's that big commission check

from the Conzalez job?" The first mate's grin widened, but quickly disappeared when he saw that Shark didn't share his amusement.

Shark began to open it carefully, so as not to mistakenly tear any of the correspondence. He unfolded the single sheet of thick parchment and read the following:

Captain Shark,

I reach out to you in anticipated friendship and with great interest. You come highly recommended. Please know that I in no way work for or represent a certain Cuban importer in Miami.

I invite you and Mr. Peeler to meet me at 524 Dunlap Neck Road, Guild Harbor, in order to hear out a business proposition. We have a mutual friend who thinks the world of you, and if you don't like what I have to offer, you can simply walk away. Your whereabouts will be immediately forgotten.

I will plan to see you tonight at 6 p.m.

In the unfortunate event that you need to send your regrets, please pass them along immediately to Sergeant Anthony O'Doul at the GHPD.

Sincerely,

Captain Jib Scola

Shark's eyes rose from the letter and looked toward the deepwater channel as a majestic fifty-foot Post Sportfish crawled by, leaving a ripple for a wake.

"What's it say, Skip?" asked an eager Peeler.

"I dunno exactly, Peel. But it looks like somebody is offering us a job of some kind. I mean, my first instinct is to burn this letter and find a new marina to hole up in. Maybe Downeast Maine? I dunno. The only thing is, while financially we're *okay*, it's not like we couldn't use the money."

"Yeah, but, Shark, ain't we lookin' good? I mean, we sold some of Conzalez's dope in Montauk. You know, the stuff we were *supposed* to give to the Don. I know that it was only a sample that we brought up that day, but don't we have enough cash from that to let us kinda just hang out for a while? Plus, we don't exactly know the waters up here. Definitely not good enough to run an operation."

Peeler sounded uncharacteristically concerned.

"Don't worry about the waters up here, Peel. In the end, they're all the same. Wet."

Shark smirked.

"Regarding finances, I said we're *okay*, but the money from my New York contact was not nearly the usual score. He could smell fear like you can sniff out ten-cent perfume. He knew we were on the run and needed to dump the shit. As a result, we got pennies on the friggin' dollar. I'm sure the prick was chuckling all the way back to Queens on the LIE. That said, with all that went down leading up to the sale, we're damn lucky we got what we did, and avoided being hung from a bridge over the A1A. My only regret is that we didn't bring more of that powdered treasure up during that first dive before you decided to murder our employer's niece."

"Shark! I had to do that! She had a gun pointed at you—"

"I'm kidding, Peel. We were in a rough spot and you did as I woulda expected. Anyway, regarding our financial status, we're *stable,* but not flush. My gut tells me we should go see this guy. If we're gonna be adrift and still on the run for the foreseeable future, we're gonna need cash. Most of my employment connections are in Florida and Bahamian waters, and we don't dare set a southerly course. Plus, if this guy's intentions were nasty, he would have just blown up our boat while we slept last night."

"All right, Skip. Whatever you say. I'm in," said Peeler, ever loyal.

"Good answer. Whaddya say we go eat? Gotta love the Spillway. They stuff a whole fillet into that chowder bowl."

"Sounds great," said Peeler. "Hope they gut it first."

CHAPTER NINE

Roll Call, Guild Harbor Police Headquarters

Unlike many of her power-addicted colleagues, Captain Mary-Louise Washington of the Guild Harbor Police Department never liked morning roll call, a requirement of her new job. She always found the vibe in the room to be annoying. In the front few rows were the eager new recruits looking to take a bite out of crime with their morning caffeine buzz, whereas the back of the hall found the seasoned veterans still picking sleep crud out of their eyes.

While a black woman being promoted to the rank of police captain in an old New England city was not totally unheard of, it sat up there with a hole-in-one in terms of frequency.

However, Louie—as she not only liked but *insisted* on being called—came up by the book and did it in a relatively short time. Some old-school skeptics made snide remarks that she was on the fast track just so the powers that be could earn political correctness points, but the officers who had worked the streets with Louie knew otherwise.

While she grew up just north of Boston in the rough, coastal city of Lynn, she had many fond childhood memories of Guild Harbor. Her father was a career swordfisherman who had labored long and hard to keep his four children in school, on track, and out of trouble. Her mom had died of heart failure while giving birth to her youngest brother. This left Louie, the oldest of four and the only daughter, to tend to the many household chores and motherly duties.

Her father's sister moved in with the family to help stabilize the day-to-day living conditions of the suddenly motherless household. But with her aunt making only a feeble attempt due to her love of Beefeater Gin, Louie soon rose to the rank of matriarch, often having to make the hard decisions and deal with challenging situations while her dad was two hundred miles offshore chasing a living at his brutal occupation.

One afternoon after a typical day as a junior at Lynn English High School, Louie heard the doorbell ring. This was strange, for Louie had a rule about no visitors during the school week, as her brothers were supposed to be either tackling practice dummies on the football field or math problems at the library.

She opened the door to behold the oldest of her three brothers and his best friend in the company of a tall, pretty redheaded female police officer. A male officer stood behind her and remained silent, taking notes and sporadically tending to his radio.

"Mary-Louise Washington?" asked the female officer.

"Yes, but please call me Louie."

"Okay, Lenny. It appears that your brother and his pal here were caught paying your neighbor to slide the brick."

"Oh, no. Not again," said Louie, rolling her eyes. That made twice this month he'd fallen down the same hole of bad behavior.

The officer continued. "Miss, I take it that you know what this offense entails?"

"Yes, Officer," Louie said. "Is my brother in any real trouble?"

Louie knew that Pete LeBoeuf down the street was forever the entrepreneur. His latest cash cow was charging the other kids in the neighborhood a dollar to stand outside his house and slide a loose brick out of the wall. This simple flaw in the construction of the modest three-decker home revealed Pete's nineteen-year-old sister relishing her daily shower after a full day of dull classes at Salem State.

The officer continued. "Nah, we're not bringing either of 'em in. Waste of time and paper. They just need to learn some manners and understand that voyeurism is a crime, not to mention just plain rude."

Louie was impressed with how the officer remained in command and professional despite the ridiculous situation. She was even more impressed that the two youths remained respectful and kept their mouths shut during the exchange. Usually these two hooligans weren't even this quiet when they were asleep.

Louie's brother spoke up. "But Louie, Pete was offering a deal. It's usually ten seconds for a buck, but today, for an extra dollar, you got half a minute! You shoulda seen—"

Louie put her hand up and shook her head in frustration. "Please leave them with me, Officer. I'll speak to them."

"Great. G'won in, fellahs, and keep it in your trousers," said the redheaded officer.

The two boys walked slowly past Louie and down the hallway, most likely to sneak out the back door and hide in the woods.

"Officer, I'm impressed that you were able to keep those two clowns in line. Must be cool to be a policewoman. Could I do that job someday? I mean, you got any black girls on the force?"

"Not many, but we got a couple. And of course you could do the job. The chief don't care if you're black, white, purple, or blue. Just so long as you don't mind chasing after Peepin' Toms in the middle of the aft'noon. G'day, Lenny. C'mon, Rodgah, let's go get a donut. You're buyin'."

And with that simple exchange, Louie decided that someday she would be a cop. Years later, she still couldn't explain exactly why, but it had something to do with the level of respect that the woman had garnered that day from two otherwise incorrigible mischief magnets.

Back at the Guild Harbor police station, Captain Washington approached the podium and raised her hands in the air to quell the chatter of the two dozen officers that were her audience.

"Morning, folks. Let's get started. As you all know, summer is approaching—that time of year when our quiet little city tends to perk up. We're gonna have the usual tourist hassles, like public drunkenness, scuffles, and peeing behind trees. Let's keep things in order while also realizing that these pests keep a lot of our locals in business," said Louie, to a few head nods.

"The St. Anthony's Festival is coming up, a chance for a lot of you to snag some overtime. Go nuts. The mayor just bumped up our budget with an early Christmas gift, courtesy of the state tourism bureau. Some city councilor in Newburyport got nabbed with his hand in the cookie jar, so we're gettin' a chunk of their summer allocation."

That little piece of information drew sly smiles, especially from the back of the room.

"Anyway, that's the usual blah-blah. Now, we need to address what the hell's *really* been goin' on," said Louie.

A few of the newer officers straightened their posture.

"As you all know, we've had some unusual occurrences within the past week, and they need to be addressed so we know what to look for while out on the street. First, we had another heroin OD death on board a fishing vessel, which makes three in the last six months. I don't like the math. While it's mostly an issue for the Coast Guard, we need to be aware that there's a lot of powder out there on the street. Unfortunately for these junkies, the dope they're getting is not nearly as pure as they anticipate. We all know it's being cut with fentanyl, which is the Grim Reaper for many of these poor bastards."

"Captain," said a new recruit in the second row. "You want us to patrol the docks more closely for the next few months?"

"We'll get to that in a minute, Sully," responded Louie. "First, we also had a floater, or should I say, part of a body, wash up in Folly Cove over the weekend. Some tourist tripped over the damn head and nearly had a coronary. The medical examiner's office has yet to release the official findings, but the prelims identified him as a local drug user who must have fallen in the drink and drowned. Looks like the crabs and sharks lined up for a buffet."

Louie paused and took a sip of water before continuing.

"While all of that is indeed tragic, the real matter on our hands occurred early yesterday morning. Some of you might not be aware of this yet, but in an alley off Main Street, some kids found the body of Casino McSurl. You all knew Casino as a local dealer with nine lives. Well, looks like Casino's ninth was finally cashed out. His body was found with a package that at first glance looked like a kilo of smack."

Some of the officers were slightly shaking their heads. Casino was a pain in the ass and a plague on the community, but it was unlike him to not be careful during an operation. He must have let his guard down for some reason.

"Casino's throat was cut," Louie continued, "and the heroin turned out to be some kinda sugar. The package was partially sliced open and left with the body. Whoever did this knew to plan the deal for an area where there were no cameras, so needless to say the perp got away with the purchase money and bragging rights to a most likely unsolvable murder."

A veteran officer spoke up. "Captain, that seems weird for around here. Think we got someone new in town? Maybe enjoyin' their summer vacation away from Dorchester?"

Louie paused before answering.

"We don't know yet. Folks, there'll be more to come on all of the above. For today, just be aware of what's around you, keep your eyes open, and dammit, look out for one another. Roll safe out there."

With that Louie gathered her papers and checked her phone for e-mails. While she had to alert her officers to get everyone on the same page, she wasn't ready to share her information just yet regarding the new enemy that was about to ride into town.

CHAPTER TEN

Home of Jib Scola, Dunlap Neck

Shark and Peeler got out of the Uber at the address included in the note from earlier in the day. Shark thanked and tipped the driver, then motioned to Peeler to start walking toward the door. He suddenly felt underdressed as they approached the house, which was a veritable mansion with all of the trimmings of a medieval castle, right up to the gargoyles staring at him from above the doorway.

"Well, Peel, we've been hired by some odd ducks before, but this time it looks like King Arthur is requesting our services."

"Yeah, Skip. Place looks like a Disney ride."

As they walked up the meandering stone path, one half of the enormous oaken door slowly opened before they even had a chance to knock.

The two salts were greeted by a pretty yet unassuming woman who Shark guessed was in her mid-forties. She waited for the men to walk up the final few steps before speaking.

"Welcome, gentlemen. My name is Amina. I work for Captain Scola, who is eagerly awaiting your arrival."

"Great. I apologize that we're a little late. At the moment we are a bit transportationally challenged. Quite a place you have here."

"Yes, Captain Scola is fortunate, indeed. I look after the house in all of its grandeur and uniqueness," said Amina, directing a semi-flirtatious smile at Captain Shark.

Shark responded with a slow nod. "Looks like this place is loaded with both."

"Please come in," she said, as she gestured toward the foyer.

As the two sea dogs walked through the hallway toward the back of the mansion, Shark experienced a sense of déjà vu from the year before, when he'd been escorted through the opulent Bal Harbour penthouse of Don Juan Conzalez.

Shark marveled at the museum-like artwork with its thick colors and dramatic depictions. The career captain admittedly knew nothing about art, but correctly guessed that none of the works were cheap. Shark smiled at the amusing thought that perhaps some of the paintings were stolen.

Shark stopped and stared for a moment at what appeared to be an old executioner's ax that hung on the wall. He noticed the rust-colored residue at the end of the dark gray blade and wondered if it was dried blood.

As Amina led the two guests into the vast harbor-view study, Shark guessed that it was their host who was tending to the fireplace.

"Gentlemen. Thank you so much for indulging my invitation. I'm Captain Jib Scola."

The three men exchanged greetings as Amina offered the guests drinks.

Peeler, as usual, spoke up first when it came to a bar call. "Ah, ma'am, I'd love a beer. Or maybe a rum and soda?"

To which Amina politely replied, "Sir, I shall bring you one of each. And you, Captain?"

"Yes, just a ginger ale with cranberry."

Amina indicated her understanding with a slight bow and left the room to fetch the order.

Captain Jib spoke first. "You don't drink when discussing business, Captain. I admire that."

"Actually, Captain Scola, when it comes to the grape, let's just say that record needle has scratched my vinyl from too many dances."

"I see. Please sit down. I know it's a warm evening, but I still love the look and smell of a fire. You'd be surprised how cool it can get out here at night, even during the warmer months, especially with an easterly breeze." Scola paused. "And please, call me Jib."

Shark and Peeler couldn't stop looking through the massive sea of glass that was the study's window, revealing an endless view of the now-peaceful Guild Harbor waters. The sun's intensity was starting to fade, and the Atlantic was taking on that certain shade of midnight blue found only when early summer days bid farewell.

"Jib, this is quite the place. Looks like Camelot Court, although at first glance you don't seem like the history professor type," remarked Shark.

"Funny story," said a smiling Jib. "I bought this place as is about a year ago. It was owned by a wealthy, local eccentric who never married or had children. He was an heir to the fortune of a prominent North Shore family dating back to the Salem–China shipping trade during the late eighteenth century. Many of the items that adorn these walls came from exotic ports around the world. This place is supposedly filled with rare artifacts and valuable curiosities, although I've no idea what the stuff is worth."

Shark nodded, genuinely impressed.

"Anyway, the guy died and left the place to his butler, who just wanted cash to get outta Dodge. Rumor has it that he may have fast-forwarded his employer's demise—you'll find this town is ripe with legends. I dunno, someday I'll ask this cutie I know at the Peabody Essex Museum to come and look around, tell me what all this shit is. I bought the place just 'cause I thought it was cool and it was on the fast track to sell. I've lived in glorified fishing shacks my whole life, thought it was time for a change."

Shark's gaze continued to take in the room. So far, he liked Jib Scola.

"Well, Jib, you got enough open space in these rooms. Shit, how high are these ceilings?"

"On the first floor, fifteen feet. More like ten on the top two floors. I severely dislike confined spaces. Some might call it acute claustrophobia. Started when I was a kid," said the host as he sipped his drink.

"Captain Shark, I'm sure you're curious as to why I asked you here tonight."

"Yeah, Jib, it crossed my mind. More pressing is my wanting to know how you found me—or how you even knew I existed?"

Amina returned with a tray of drinks and set it down in front of the guests. Peeler's gaze changed from boredom to excitement as he looked at the tray like a winning lottery ticket. He selected the rum first. He figured he'd need to grease the wheels quickly to handle this strange situation.

"If that will be all, Captain?" asked the maid. "I'm going to head out."

"Thank you, Amina. That will be all for now," said Jib as he took a glass of scotch and sat back and looked at Shark.

As usual, Peeler's wandering eyes followed Amina's exit. "Hey Jib, she's cute. She your girlfriend?"

"No, Mr. Peeler. Amina came to me shortly after I bought the place. She had heard through word of mouth that I'd made the purchase and inquired as to my household upkeep needs. I will admit that at first I had ulterior motives, but she has never in any way suggested such an arrangement. She keeps to herself, goes out at night to her community meetings, and then I have no idea what she does. She has her own quarters here at the house, but I don't know which nights she stays and which nights she doesn't return until dawn, in order to prepare my breakfast. Must have a boyfriend in town or something, I dunno."

Peeler tilted his head and curved his lips as if to say "That's too bad."

"Anyway, Captain, as I mentioned, it seems that you and I have a mutual friend who highly recommended you," said Jib. "A certain Bostonian named Justin McGee."

Shark's eyes lit up. While he thought of his former business partner every day, aside from the occasional mention from Peeler, he had not heard that name spoken in almost a year.

Jib continued. "I can tell by your look, Captain Shark, that you're surprised I know this individual. I'm happy that you know him as McGee and not Tom Baxter, like many of his more-recent acquaintances. He must have trusted you?"

Shark paused. "Yeah, funny you should mention that. When I was first introduced to him, he went by Baxter, but after a while he told me to call him Justin. Weird. I never really got an explanation, and as close as we were, I've never known the whole story about his background. I certainly knew some of it, but I always felt like he was withholding some details."

Jib rubbed at his two-day stubble. "Justin had an illustrious career in Boston. He's now officially on the lam from the Boston

FBI, as well as from several other law enforcement agencies. You see, Justin McGee was an assassin for hire, and quite a successful and prolific one at that."

Shark's eyes lit up at this bit of information.

"He operated below the radar for several years," Jib said, "until he finally pushed the envelope and blasted a long-range rifle bullet into an assistant district attorney."

"Wow—holy shit" was all Shark could mutter.

"Oh, it gets better. I take it that you may have met Justin's lady friend during your time together?"

"Of course—Marlene. She's fantastic on operations. She keeps Justin reined in just enough so we don't take unnecessary risks. Kind of a mother hen to all of us at times," laughed Shark.

"Yeah, well, said *hen* is the assistant district attorney whose head Justin tried to blow clean off back in Boston."

Jib was enjoying the look of profound shock on both of the men's faces.

"I'll be *damned!*" said Shark. "He tried to kill *Marlene?*"

"Indeed. And the employer who hired him for that particular contract has not forgotten McGee's rare lack of success on that particular hit. His name is Darby McBride, and last I heard, he's hot on the hunt for McGee. Typical of Jus, he somehow keeps eluding him."

Shark was trying to process this multilevel information all at once.

"Man, that must have happened after we all parted ways last year. Wait, wait! Hold on, this makes no sense. You're telling me that my friend Justin shoots Marlene, who then ends up with him while they hide out in a marina? Then, some Paddy gangster tracks him down? This is insane. I mean—well, damn, where are they now?"

"I couldn't venture a guess at the moment," responded Jib. He took a sip of scotch. "Anyway, he mentioned you in an e-mail recently, saying that he thought you would be heading north. He even gave me a detailed description of your vessel. I've kept my eyes and ears open, as I know every boat sitting in these marinas. I asked around and finally you appeared. It must be some kind of divine intervention, 'cause now's the time I could use you the most."

"That is *messed up*," Shark said, only half concentrating. His mind was still processing some of Jib's story. "I mean, I didn't know Justin for all that long, but the two of us, and eventually Marlene, ended up getting involved in more than our share of operations together. Mostly dull counterfeiting gigs, but our last job together involved human livery and terrorist shit. Man, it was a cluster-F."

Shark was rarely thrown for a loop, but clearly he was still struggling with the memories of that operation. Finally, he grabbed ahold of himself.

"Why am I telling you *anything* about my past?" Shark said. "For all I know, you're FBI. You seem to know an awful lot about everyone and everything."

"At the risk of sounding cliché, Shark, we both know that knowledge is power."

Shark exhaled. "Okay, Jib. Why are we here? Why us? Cliffs Notes version, please."

"Yes, I do owe you that. Let's just say that about five or six years ago I had an epiphany, at a time when many men go through such things. Midlife crisis, as many inaccurately dub it; in reality, it was a period of reassessment.

"Life as I knew it was quickly ceasing to exist. While I consider myself a formidable fisherman in a formidable town, there was no denying the fact that the fish stocks were being depleted. Some media outlets blamed advances in commercial fishing technologies, which provided a greater catch amount in shorter periods of time, while other theories lay the blame on increased governmental regulation and intervention. Personally, I'd say it's an equal combination of the two. Follow me so far, gentlemen?"

"Clear as mud, Jib. Similar stories all up and down the East Coast," said Shark.

Peeler drained his rum glass while reaching for the beer Amina had served.

Jib continued. "At the same time that my professional life was being compromised by various factors, my personal life also began to erode. Over time, my wife, who I adored, decided that the life of a Guild Harbor fisherman's wife was not to her satisfaction, nor was I, for that matter. She put her lawyer's business card under a magnet on the fridge and left with an overnight bag."

"Sorry to hear that, Jib. That sucks. I guess we both know that holding a maritime marriage together is like pulling a barge against a riptide."

"Good analogy, Shark. Anyway, I don't blame her, but the pain was real, and I needed to spark some alterations to my lifestyle. I knew

I had a large network of contacts in town, and I knew the Cape Ann offshore waters better than any nautical chart designer. I also felt like I wanted a little action—and a lotta money."

Shark rubbed his chin. "So, you fancied getting into the *transport* field. And maybe your cargo didn't always consist of canned goods or citrus from down south? I'd say in order to buy a house like this, you would have needed a foray into the shipment of products that were a little more in demand and difficult to procure via traditional methods."

Jib nodded. "In order to hit the real scores, I began running contraband. It started with various product lines, but as you now, all roads lead to heroin. And lots of it."

"Wow," said Shark. "You get right to the point."

"You gettin' any younger, Skipper?" asked Scola.

Shark rubbed his chin some more and began to pace. "It's sad to think back. I often reminisce about those supposedly innocent days of running weed from Mexico, around the Straits of Florida. Those were creampuff runs, and the players at the table didn't wield automatic weapons. Once coke and smack became the products du jour, we could transport a lot more at one time, and of course the greed and danger increased accordingly."

Jib nodded in agreement. "And to make matters more complicated, Captain Shark, over the past few years we've learned how to cut the product with other, shall we say, *additives*, such as talc, low-grade coke, and the granddaddy of them all, fentanyl. As you know, *that* was the real game-changer. Demand went through the roof. A friggin' month's worth of product could fit into a sea bag that you could toss in the cuddy of a day cruiser. Gone were the days of dozens of bales of weed filling up the holds of big commercial fishing vessels that were constantly under Coast Guard scrutiny.

"But then we had a problem, which is why you and Peeler have been invited here tonight. Once fentanyl was introduced into the mix, yes, profits exploded, but the number of overdoses increased at a commensurate pace.

"None of this will surprise you, Captain Shark. Guild Harbor is a town famous for looking the other way on many fronts, but we stop short at dead kids."

The room was silent. Shark's wheels were visibly turning in his head.

"So, Jib, I take it that the heat under your burner has been turned up, but not by your own hand. You want to bow out before someone *takes* you out? Perhaps some community-minded vigilante?" asked Shark.

"Pretty much," responded Jib. "I recently received my first bona fide death threat, and I didn't like it. The reason my father and his father before him both perished at sea was that they never knew when enough was enough. Sometimes, it's time to weigh anchor, head back to port, and be satisfied with a day's catch—not get too greedy. I'm at that place now."

"Your story is interesting, Jib, and unfortunately very common up and down the East Coast for guys in our profession. But why get me involved? Why not just hand the boat keys to some young maverick, sell this joint, and head to Bermuda, bring that cute housekeeper with you? Why are you overcomplicating things—unless there's something you're not telling me?"

"I could easily do that. Just pick up and scram. However, I have two partners involved in the operation. One is a mariner, like us, and one is crooked law enforcement, which comes in handy, as you know. We've all done well, but we have an opportunity to make one last score, of such magnitude that we'll be set for life—or at least the span of time worth living. I'm not too concerned about what age ninety will look like for me financially. I wouldn't mind skipping the catheter years."

Shark was quickly catching on, but wanted clarification.

"So what service can Peeler and I provide for you that you can't do yourself? And what's in it for us?"

"Captain Shark, I have no idea what your financial situation looks like, but I assume that being on the run and not scoring can get rather expensive over time?"

Shark smirked. "Your assumption is correct, Jib. Also, I don't like playing on the defensive side of the ball for too long. It makes one rusty and dimwitted over time. Like a Thoroughbred, I can always use an occasional run around the track, and I wouldn't mind a few bucks for my trouble. Tell me more."

"The FDA recently approved a new drug that you most likely have never heard of, called Tsulio. It was designed specifically for military use, for wounded soldiers on the battlefield, but we've learned that it's ten times more powerful than fentanyl, which, if you do the math, is already one hundred times more powerful than morphine. I have a shipment of the stuff due to come in from Nova Scotia. I'll be the first prick in New England to enjoy the biggest smack score to ever hit the East Coast. I plan to combine the Tsulio with a typical shipment of brown. We'll cut the shit a thousand ways to Sunday, and sell it all over the coast from Cape Cod to Bar Harbor. Western New England dealers from as far away as Vermont and even upstate New York will trek across the Mass Pike like Ethan Allen to stock up."

Shark shook his head in disbelief at the sheer magnitude of the run.

"The thing is, Shark, I can't just go out and get it. I have to assume that whoever is sending me death threats has their eyes all over my Guinea ass. What I need is someone unknown to quietly blast offshore in the middle of the night, meet up with some reliable Canadian fisherman types who I've dealt with for years, pick up the shipment, and bring it right back to your slip in town. We'll move the bundles like we're unloading a week's halibut catch right under everyone's noses. Nobody notices a thing.

"Then, we gather up all the product at my partner Eel's warehouse, estimate the value of the take, and you and Mr. Peeler here take ten percent of the gross in a shopping bag and get the hell out of our sight with the next ebbing tide."

Shark scratched his head while Peeler looked on.

"So, Jib, this figure of ten percent of the gross—is that a fair slice? I mean, with this Tsulio being a new product and all, why can't you let out the sails a little more?"

Jib calmly responded, "Shark, all you gotta do is make the pickup, bring it to the marina, come to a warehouse two miles away, and collect your bag. No nonsense with the dealers. No risk of street exposure, no raids, and, most importantly, no dead bodies in the street. You are just off in the wind while we deal with the hard part, which will be the distribution and aftermath."

Shark tilted his head as Jib continued.

"This shipment is solid. We're gonna bring in about fifteen kilos of H, with a street value of about one-point-two million. Normally, after a cut with fentanyl, that number blasts off to a value of around three million. With the new Tsulio additive and the product's strength on steroids, the gross street-sale value will easily exceed ten million. You and Peeler walk away with a cool million, tax-free, in a suitcase. All for about twelve hours of work, and all of it light lifting compared to what you're accustomed to. Will that cover your fuel, marina hideout fees, and Chinese takeout for another year? Plus, you'll be taking part in history as members of the first Tsulio score in the Northeast Atlantic. Maybe they'll even put up a plaque someday with our names and images, if they ever figure out who pulled it off. We shake hands and part ways, and never see one another again.

"So whaddya say, Captain? You in?"

Shark was quiet, tilting his head back in thought.

"You mentioned a partner who's law enforcement. I'm assuming it's this O'Doul you mentioned in your note?" Shark asked. "How much protection can he provide, and does it extend offshore?"

"Yeah, that's him," replied Jib. "In terms of how far his protection extends, well, that could get a bit dicey. Anything involving the harbormaster can be taken care of with a brown bag. That's cake. However, if the Coast Guard gets involved, the stakes are immediately raised. It's not the 1980s anymore, especially now that they've been annexed by Homeland Security. They have a bigger budget, with an attitude to match. They're outta our reach.

"The good thing is, if you use your own vessel for the job, you're not going to attract a lot of attention. You'll look like any other weekend warrior fisherman out on a cod trip to Jeffrey's Ledge. Again, the nice thing about my product of choice is that it doesn't require a large vessel with a ton of cargo space. That said, the obvious risks still apply."

Shark was quiet. He looked at Peeler, who had finally begun to understand both the risks and rewards of this assignment. He remained quiet, as well, knowing not to interfere at this stage, and to let Shark man the helm.

"Well, Captain Jib, that's quite an offer. With the numbers you're tossing around, and the fact that you know your cover has been compromised to *some* degree, don't you think the risk of this assignment grows heavier ev'ry day?"

"That's exactly why I need to know within twenty-four hours whether or not you want in on this score."

Shark rubbed his chin. "This is a lot to consider. I'd appreciate some time to consider your offer. You'll have my answer by this time tomorrow."

"Excellent, gentlemen," said Jib, tapping his desk. He instinctively felt this was a proposal Shark couldn't resist. "I'll walk you out."

After seeing the two smugglers out of his home, Jib returned to his study, savoring the feeling of setting a hook.

CHAPTER ELEVEN

Hope Harbor Beach, Guild Harbor

Spike Mahone was gonna show 'em. He was gonna prove everyone wrong if it took until the day he died, which the doctors told him might be closer than he'd anticipated.

Yeah, the emphysema was a drag, to be sure, but he'd rather greet the Reaper than face his wife's scolding as they entered retirement way short of the funds they needed to buy a little place in Florida and get the hell out of Guild Harbor for the rest of their days. He had promised her that ten years ago, and he was woefully behind.

Spike had always assured his wife that his job as a train engineer for the Massachusetts Transit Railroad would secure them a comfortable future. Hell, he was fully vested in his pension and he would be taken care of by the union upon his retirement. His dues were current.

Martha Mahone had spent many years raising kids and cleaning up Spike's dirty dishes and ashtrays. When she asked about their financial situation, Spike would just wave his hand dismissively and tell her to stop worrying, and to fetch him another Meister Brau while she was at it.

Spike did have a decent situation if he played his cards tight to his vest. The problem was, over the years Spike had thrown a lot of cards onto a hot coal table.

What had started as an innocent poker game in his early thirties had slowly evolved into calling in sick and taking his chances with the Pequot Nation down at Connecticut's Foxwoods Casino. Spike's intentions may have been pure, but he either overestimated his ability to beat the dealers or underestimated the level of his addiction. Whatever the case, he was in the ninth inning toward retirement and finally realized that the next twenty years' worth of security lay down in the Connecticut woods.

So, like any rational gambler would tell himself, he would just find another angle. Another kind of table to conquer.

On this particular beautiful, sunburst morning Spike found himself with his metal detector combing the soft, white sands of Hope Harbor Beach. His goal was to find a tourist's lost ring, or a money clip buried in the sand, left behind by one of the hundreds of visitors from the past weekend. He always walked barefoot along the shoreline, digging his toes in the sand to make sure his mechanical partner hadn't missed anything.

He waved the metal detector back and forth along the middle section of the beach. He knew that's where the tourists would lay down their blankets and sleep off a mid-afternoon beer buzz. Not too far up toward the parking lot, the sun would blaze and dry them out by noon. They tended to set up camp not too close to the water's edge. Anything dropped or lost would be claimed by the high tide.

His right forearm swung back and forth with the device leading the way. Methodical roaming and swinging. Swinging and roaming. Some passersby would smile at his actions, while others would look away out of pity.

So far, it was turning out to be another one of those unfortunate outings devoid of any pay dirt, until suddenly the whine of the buzzer sounded off. He often chuckled at how the buzzing sound reminded him of Martha's warnings about the fate of their retirement.

Spike moved the metal detector back over the spot where he'd first caught the sound. It was obvious where the buzz was coming from, so he shut off the machine and laid down his backpack. He opened it and took out a couple of gardening tools and began digging.

A couple of local kids who'd skipped school were sitting on a nearby wall, awaiting the delivery of an ounce of weed that they'd sell during the week. They nudged one another and chuckled as they watched the crazy old beachcomber who thought he'd struck gold. They still had a decent buzz going from some of last week's stash.

Spike dug, at first thinking that maybe he'd chosen the wrong spot. Suddenly his small garden shovel hit something. He was used to hitting hard objects and having to dig around them to find a ring or a coin. This time the target was soft and gave way.

He removed the sand from around his target. Like an archaeologist, he dug carefully so as not to damage what he had found. As the sand went from the hole to the beach's topside, a human forearm was revealed.

"Holy shit," Spike muttered to himself.

He dug more and uncovered the entire arm.

He jumped back and screamed, his only audience the two stoners on the wall.

Spike stood up and stepped back, assessing the situation.

The metal detector hadn't picked up the signal of a watch or a ring, but rather the metal of a needle stuck in the middle of the decaying flesh.

CHAPTER TWELVE

Kelsey's Bar, Guild Harbor

"Hey, Madge, another Caucasian when you have a chance," said Eel Korvitz from his usual perch at the far end of Kelsey's Bar. Monday night was when the usuals gathered to talk about the weekend, gear up for *Monday Night Football* when in season, order takeout from Vinny's, and, more importantly, get a jump on another week's worth of bad-habit drinking.

"Hey, Slip, did you order from Vinney's yet? I'm *stahvin'*."

"Yeah, Eel, just got you the usual. Should be here soon," replied Slip, whose real name was Fred Torkinton.

Poor Slip had been a drinking buddy of Eel's since their days at Guild Harbor High School. He'd been a handsome student and star athlete until one night, after drinking a plastic bottle of Popov vodka stolen from his father's liquor closet, he'd lost his footing on the wet rocks of a jetty on the Annisquam River. He had tumbled down ten feet onto a washed-up lobster trap. A piece of the gear ended up claiming his left eye, which had to be replaced with what was basically a cat's-eye marble. Slip refused to wear a patch, frightening those who made eye contact with him on his left side, where he always appeared to be looking away. Local lore said that the maritime medics who had treated him inserted a compass in the prosthetic so that no matter which way he faced, his left eye was always looking toward the North Pole.

Eel asked Madge, "You mind turning the station? Let's try and catch tomorrow's weather. Might go fishing."

"Yeah, hold on," said Madge. She placed a fresh White Russian on a napkin in front of Eel and then grabbed the remote control, which stuck to her hand from a weekend's worth of spilled drinks.

Eel watched the pearly white smile on the screen deliver the headlines.

In local news, residents and tourists alike are still in shock over the discovery of the remains of a man on Cape Ann over the weekend. The usually quiet Folly Cove was rocked by the discovery of human remains found by a sunbather late Sunday morning. The cause of death remains suspicious. Nancy Preston has more from Guild Harbor . . .

Eel was transfixed. He felt the reporter was fixated directly on him as she delivered an on-location report and read the gruesome details from the teleprompter as the late-spring wind blew through her auburn hair. He knew damn well what had happened to the guy. While Eel had enjoyed the smuggling runs that he and Jib had pulled off over the past few years, the body count was getting too high. He'd been warning Jib for months now that they were getting too big for their britches.

A quiet murmur was growing on the streets about who was behind the recent influx of deadly fentanyl-laced heroin plaguing the community. Eel knew about Jib's plans for one last big score that would hopefully allow them to retire for good. That is, if they weren't taken out by some vigilante first. *Somebody* knew what they were up to; the question remained—who was it, and how much did they know?

"Hey, Eel, food's here," said Slip, handing the delivery guy cash for their order. He brought the large bag over to where the group was sitting and tossed it on the bar.

"Okay, who's got the veal with no sauce?"

Already nervous by nature, Eel was starting to unravel from the stress and pressure associated with the drug-smuggling operation. He started to sweat during even the most mundane conversations, he'd been drinking more, and he was doing absentminded things like forgetting where he'd parked his car.

Unlike his partner Jib, who had bought a castle by the sea that housed a classic car collection and a cute maid, Eel had tried to be smart with his newfound wealth, maintaining the modest lifestyle he'd enjoyed throughout his life. He kept his cash tucked away in safe deposit boxes as close as Manchester-by-the-Sea and as far away as Orleans, Cape Cod. He even stashed a hundred thousand in an antique gumball machine in his elderly aunt's attic, on her small farm in nearby Hamilton.

To many, Eel gave off the appearance of someone who is slightly dim. He played the role of shy and unassuming, someone who simply played by the rules. He was confident that his prudence would lead to his long-term survival even as his partner attracted unwanted attention and envy.

Growing up in Guild Harbor, he had run with Jib Scola since the two were in first grade. Jib was always the action seeker and risk-taker while Eel had always been happy to ride in the sidecar. At times, Eel's shyness had given other kids an opportunity to poke fun at his awkward mannerisms, such as engaging in full-blown discussions with himself as he walked alone down the street, calling him *dimwit*, *retard*, and even *crab brain*. When the other kids would tease him, Eel would merely look away or turn in the other direction. It was always Jib who would grab him by the collar and lead him back to confront the cruel taunter.

One day when Eel was eight years old, he was walking with a bucket of crabs that he'd caught by flipping over some rocks at low tide in Loblolly Cove. He was heading home to show his mother what he had found, in hopes that she would cook them up for supper. He knew she'd probably tell him to go down to the creek and release them, back to the sea.

"Would you like some little prick plucking you out of your home only to toss you into a pot of boiling water?" Eel's mother would scold him. Little did she know there were days when Eel wished for just that.

As he walked up the rocky road, staring into the sloshing pail, he heard footsteps behind him. It was Todd Grogan and some kid named Mitch, Grogan's lackey for that particular summer. Grogan's dad was high up in the Guild Harbor police, well liked within the community, and thus the kid felt he was above the law when it came to punishment and consequences.

As the three boys met on the rock path, Eel put down the bucket and waited for Grogan and Mitch to approach.

"What you got there, dummy boy?" asked the always antagonistic Grogan.

"Just some crabs I caught down da cove. I'm gonna bring 'em

home and have my ma cook 'em up for dinnah," Eel replied nervously.

Grogan peered into the bucket.

"Well, Mitch, look what we have here. Green crabs. Maybe a dozen?"

Mitch just stood silently in Grogan's shadow and chuckled when cued to do so.

"Hey, Eel, you know what? These are special crabs. They can fly," said the young bully.

"They ain't for flyin', Grogan," Eel shot back. "They're for *suppah*."

"Let me show you, retard boy. I'll show you something really special."

Grogan produced a pack of firecrackers out of his pocket and with his other hand took a crab out of the pail.

Eel was starting to panic. "You leave them alone! I'll get you into trouble!"

Grogan laughed and looked at Mitch. "No, you won't. You know who my dad is."

Grogan shoved the firecracker into the crab's mouth. "When I light the match, he'll go off like a rocket."

Eel was too frozen with nerves to do anything.

When Grogan lit the fuse, both firecracker and crab exploded into a hundred pieces.

Eel was on the verge of tears.

"Oops," said Grogan. "I said he would fly. Here, let's try another."

Eel grabbed the bucket and all three boys began to tussle. Eel was at a clear disadvantage until he saw two hands grab Grogan's shoulders and shove him to the ground. The same person then kicked the bully twice in the stomach.

"Grogan, you piece of shit! I don't care if your daddy *is* a cop— you're a piece of shit! You ever bother my friend again, I'll shove that whole pack of firecrackers straight up your ass and light them with my dad's flamethrower. Now, get the fuck outta here. Go!"

Mitch was already running down the road in the other direction as Grogan slowly got up and limped away.

A young Jib Scola looked at Eel as he brushed him off.

"Man, I told you to stay away from those guys. Grogan's the worst kind of bully. Deep down he's just scared and wimpy. Look at him. Fell to the ground like a dead bird out of a nest. C'mon, I'll follow you home, 'case they come back."

Years later, as Grogan got older and finally graduated from Guild Harbor High School, the schoolyard scuffles had escalated into violent melees involving serious injuries, which led to arrests and weapons charges. His parents had retired full-time to Florida, and without his father there to provide protection, the street punk had had to fend for himself. He took up scuba diving, and became known for pilfering lobster traps owned by local lobstermen who had plied their trade for generations.

After Grogan had stolen one bug too many, they found him one morning tangled in scuba gear under a pile of cinder blocks dropped on him while he was underwater. One of the blocks had been used to smash in the right side of Grogan's head.

Eel was jerked back to the present at Kelsey's Bar.

"Eel, ain't you chicken with extra provolone, light sauce? Here ya go," said Slip, sliding the wrapped sub down toward Eel.

Eel was starving. Excessive nerves always made him hungry, although his third White Russian was helping to calm his mood.

Eel grabbed a couple of napkins from the metal box on the bar and prepared to enjoy his weekly barside feast. When he opened the wrapper he noticed a unique smell wafting from the sandwich. He didn't think much of it until he'd rolled the sub onto the paper plate. What he uncovered was not his usual Monday-night meal. Lying in the midst of a sea of melted cheese was a large brown sand eel. He leaned back on the barstool, aghast. As he looked more closely he realized that the eel in the sandwich was missing its head.

Eel clenched a fist and jabbed it against his closed mouth, exhaling slowly. He felt a panic attack coming on and was utilizing one of the coping techniques his counselor had taught him.

The other guys noticed the sudden change in his demeanor and looked at his plate.

Slip finally called over to the bartender. "Madge, better get Eel another Caucasian."

CHAPTER THIRTEEN

Guild Harbor Police Headquarters

Despite some of the unnerving activity occurring in town lately, Captain Mary-Louise Washington was enjoying a low-key morning at her desk in her private office at Guild Harbor police headquarters.

While most cops abhorred the mountains of paperwork, which despite modern technological advances in police work were still a well-ingrained part of the job, Louie found the shuffling and methodical signing of her name therapeutic and relaxing. While it was not yet technically summer, Guild Harbor was already starting to feel the reach of the outside world as it began to infiltrate the peaceful community.

As Louie began compiling files into some semblance of order, her thoughts drifted back to when she had assumed family laundry duty after her mother had died. She would always greet her dad with kisses and hugs when he came through the door after an especially long swordfishing trip. In turn, he would toss on the floor two large sea bags full of dirty clothes that reeked of the filthiest alley behind a sardine cannery.

She remembered how her brothers would run at the sight of the two totes, leaving the job to Louie. At first she felt frustrated, being stuck with the extra dirty work, but when the clothes were all finally clean and dry, she took pride in her accomplishment and enjoyed the relaxation that came with the simple folding and arranging of her father's garments. She also valued the sense of order she could bestow upon his otherwise tumultuous life, both personal and professional. It was as if each side of her dad's world was always trying to ride out a gale.

As Louie was finishing up approving last month's overtime report, Officer Stanger knocked on her door.

"Captain Washington, you have a visitor. She doesn't have an appointment, but she's eager to see you. I told her you were busy, but I get the feeling you might want her to come in."

"What is this about, Officer?"

"It's the mother of the kid who overdosed recently on that fishing vessel. She's pretty upset. I guess I could tell her to—"

"No, no, please bring her in," said Louie.

"Yes, Captain," said Stanger, who left to retrieve the visitor.

Louie hated these meetings. It was bad enough that loved ones are always left behind asking questions and swimming in guilt. Many ended up at the police station looking for answers as if there was some secret key to unlock the reasons why addicts spiral out of control. Unfortunately for those left behind, the driving forces are rarely ever discovered.

Officer Stanger opened the door and ushered the grieving mother into the room and over to the chair facing Louie's desk. The police captain stood and greeted the woman.

"Good morning, ma'am. I'm Captain Washington. Please have a seat."

The woman sat and placed her bag next to the chair, running her fingers through her hair and rubbing her forehead.

"Thanks for seeing me with no notice. My name is Claudette Selkirk. I'm sure you're busy getting ready for the summer rush and all, so I won't take much of your time."

"It's no problem at all, Mrs. Selkirk. I'm sorry for your loss. This was a tragedy. From what I understand, your son was adored by his fellow crew members."

Claudette shrugged her shoulders. "I guess. Don't mean much now." She looked like she had a thought, but it quickly passed as she cleared her throat.

"I'm here, Captain, because I want to know what the police are doing about these kids sticking needles in their arms and falling over dead. I been in this town my whole life—that's over fifty years—and while it's always had its demons, I ain't never seen nothing like this."

Louie was quiet, as she knew the epidemic was going to get worse.

"Mrs. Selkirk, it's never easy for any of us in these situations. At yesterday's roll call, I briefed my officers on what's been going on.

For better or worse, most of them have been touched firsthand by addiction in one form or another. You can trust they are out there trying to get to the bottom of it."

Claudette suddenly snapped. "Yeah, but that ain't enough! If we were in fucking Manchester or Marblehead, they'd have the goddamned army in the streets and the navy in the hahbah! Ya know, trying to find out what the hell is going on and where it's—" Claudette paused midstream. "I-I'm sorry."

"No need to apologize, Mrs. Selkirk. Your son was a brave man in a brutal business. I'm sure that on most occasions he made you very proud, being out there on those fishing runs."

"Yes. Yes, he did. My late husband and my father both fished their whole lives. My daddy had a nice long career. He died young, but happy. My husband was not so lucky. Gale of '07 got him while my kids were still young. Despite what happened to his father, all Simon ever wanted to do was get out on one of those damn boats. Just like so many others. To them, it looks like freedom, you know? No stop signs, no probation officers. Just the fresh ocean air and the thrill of the hunt."

Louie listened quietly. "I know that kind of guy, Mrs. Selkirk. My father was one, too."

Claudette's eyes widened. "Your father was a fisherman?"

"Yes, ma'am, right here in Guild Harbor. We lived in Lynn, but he came up here to fish. Kept comin' even after my mother passed."

Claudette paused as if afraid to ask. "Did he retire happy, like my father?"

Although she was used to answering that question, Louie bowed her head all the same.

"No, Mrs. Selkirk. Unfortunately he died shortly after I graduated high school."

"The sea always takes the good ones," Claudette said. "One way or another, they all belong to the sea and her false promises. In the beginning, during, and in the end."

CHAPTER FOURTEEN

Dunlap Neck

Jib Scola usually only slept a couple of hours at a time. If he managed to grab a couple of three-hour spurts, that was considered a success.

He was sprawled out on the oversized leather couch in his study, finally swimming in sleep. Although for Jib, sleep seldom brought solace to his ever-increasingly guilty mind.

He wandered into a dream . . .

He was at the southeasterly facing beaches on the North Shore that he'd loved to visit as a boy. That's where he could find the waves. Big waves. Waves that only came from when the blow exceeded twenty knots.

He was about twelve years old, the perfect age for riding waves and catching crabs that scurried sideways across the sand, oblivious to the twirling surf four feet above.

He jumped each roller as they invaded the shore. His body would greet the wave with chest thrust forward, only to feel weightless as he left the ground with the crest.

This was the perfect pastime for a boy who had not yet discovered girls, and had not yet been introduced to Atari. He only thought of the North Atlantic's dark blue color, challenging himself as to how high he could get with the biggest wave.

He danced in the surf and found his thoughts meandering—until he felt a bump.

"Huh?" he said to himself.

There was a smack against his left hand, meant to keep him stationary and buoyant.

A moment passed, as did another roller. He was not paying attention to the waves so he inadvertently took a slug of sea water, which made him gag.

He did not anticipate any obstacles in the water, and he was not afraid of sharks. Being brought up in Guild Harbor, you knew they were out there, but you also knew they had little interest in people.

He gathered himself and waited for the next roller.

He was treading water a little deeper than normal, so he danced from one leg to another just to achieve buoyancy. Left to right. Right to left. Little forward. Little backward. He tried to maintain position to greet the best waves as the tide began to shift.

"Damn!" he yelled.

The body of a fisherman he recognized smashed into his chest. The corpse rolled over and its vacant eyes and slack jaw looked up at him.

The tide was starting to rush. The body was pinned against his, the face incessantly staring with marble eyes devoid of all color.

It took five rings from Jib's cell phone to bring him out of his semi-trance. He turned around and reached toward his desk to pick up the cell, if only to shut the thing up.

"Scola" was all he said.

There was a pause at the other end, which after a few seconds was followed by a soft female voice.

"Mr. Scola? This is Jasmine Browne. I'm getting my doctorate in chemistry and have been mentoring your daughter since she started the semester. She's such a sweet kid, and what a promising student. She mentioned that you were looking for some research help?"

This was one call Jib was happy to receive.

"Yes, Ms. Browne. I appreciate your call. Mary Ann really admires you, and I'd like to thank you for helping her adjust to life on campus. I wouldn't know from personal experience, but I imagine being a college student must be a far cry from growing up in a fishing family."

"Well, Mr. Scola—"

"Please, call me Jib," he said.

"Okay, Jib. And please call me Jasmine."

"Fine, Jasmine. Thank you again for calling me so soon. That was a quick response."

"Well, to be honest, putting myself through undergrad and now grad school has been difficult," said Jasmine. "When Mary Ann mentioned you might have a job for me, well, I jumped at it. I love projects, and frankly, I could use a little extra money."

This was exactly what Jib wanted to hear. The hook was set.

In his own way, he was trying to get a handle on what Tsulio would do to his community after his exodus. Even Jib had his own twisted sense of morals, and it pained him to think that he was going to leave a trail of bodies in his wake. He had to get an idea of what the hurricane might bring—not that it would ever change his plans. Just curiosity, and a way to settle his soul.

"Well, Jasmine, as you know, I'm a fisherman, as were most of Mary Ann's male ancestors. We have a proud tradition up here in Guild Harbor."

"Yes, Mary Ann has told me a lot about your family's history. It's interesting, especially to a city girl from the Bronx," said Jasmine.

Few people knew that while Jasmine Browne was a first-year chemistry grad student, she was already being courted by the most sought-after international chemical and pharmaceutical companies who craved prodigies like her. She had grown up dirt poor in a tough section of the Bronx once known as Fort Apache, and had been "discovered" by her high school chemistry teacher, who had seen incredible potential in her. With a little help from his connections, and a ton of hard work on Jasmine's part, she had landed a full scholarship from Boston College to study chemistry as an undergraduate.

Now that she was in grad school, funds were not as easily available, and Jasmine found herself barely scraping by financially—although this certainly wasn't reflected in her level of focus and subsequent stellar grades. She had a gift, and Jib was about to tap into her wealth of knowledge.

"The fishing community here in Guild Harbor is looking to hire somebody for a special project, which will pay handsomely. The only catch is that it requires *absolute and total* secrecy. I mean, the level of secrecy that would exclude even Mary Ann from knowing about your efforts and your findings. Are you comfortable with that type of assignment, Jasmine?"

"Well, I guess so," Jasmine said, pausing for a moment. "But it can't be anything illegal. I've worked too hard to—"

"Jasmine, I would never engage in anything illicit," Jib said reassuringly, "nor would I ever have your good standing compromised. It's just that your findings might prove to be a bit, shall we say, controversial."

"Well, I guess that's okay," Jasmine replied. "Can you keep my name out of any reports or whatever?

I'd like to stay in the background, so to speak. Kinda been there my whole life, anyway."

"You have my word—my utmost guarantee that you will remain anonymous throughout the entire project. Anonymity is something I can understand. Unfortunately, that means you won't enjoy any credit for your hard work, but you will be well compensated financially."

Jasmine eagerly responded, "Trust me, Jib, I need cash way more than I need the limelight."

"Good," said Jib. "Allow me to explain what we need. Recently we've seen a scourge of opiate overdoses from kids in Guild Harbor who are getting involved way over their heads on some nasty stuff."

Jasmine was immediately interested. "It's not just in Guild Harbor, Jib. This goes way beyond New England."

Jib was quiet for a second. "Yes, unfortunately you are correct. That's the reason I want to commission you to help us. As a chemist, you might know how these drugs work and how we can prevent more tragedies. Jasmine, there's a new drug on the market called Tsulio. Are you familiar with it?"

The chemistry prodigy thought for a moment. "I've just heard a little buzz about it at this point, Jib. It's not really in the forefront just yet, but yeah, I've heard of it. Real nasty. Military-grade."

"Well, as you can imagine, it's only a matter of time before this drug hits the street. What I need to know is exactly *how deadly* this stuff is, and how I can best warn my fellow fishing captains about the potential for one of their crewmen to wind up facedown on a wet deck. Or worse, burning in a hot engine room. From what I understand, the chemical makeup of the drug renders it ten times more potent than fentanyl. If that's true, it's very bad news for our industry. Not just in Guild Harbor, but all up and down the East Coast.

"What I'd like is for you to research the drug and tell me if there is any way to mitigate its effects."

Jasmine thought for a moment.

"What you're looking for is most likely not available. With all due respect, it's also a bit naive to think the government would publish such information. Big Pharma has a stranglehold on Capitol Hill. Pardon my candor, but I don't think you fully understand what these drug companies are pumping out."

"No, no—I'm sure you're right. Maybe I'm grasping at straws, but that's why I want to engage your services, tap into your knowledge. I just want to know what's gonna happen when Tsulio hits the streets."

"Well," replied Jasmine, "I will research it for you, *discreetly*. But to be honest, Jib, I think you'd better make sure there's plenty of vacant land in the Guild Harbor cemetery."

CHAPTER FIFTEEN

Cape Ann Boat Basin, *Booty Call* **at berth**

The sun sparkled on the water, the ripples moving northward with the incoming tide on the Annisquam River as Captain Shark pondered his future.

Peeler, busy in the cockpit reconditioning an old trolling reel, caught a thought and looked up to make conversation with his boss, who was especially quiet this morning.

"Hey, Skip, think I'm gonna spool this up with wire. Ya know, grab us some of these Boston stripers next time we're out puttin' around."

"Don't bother, Peel. You forget where we are. Can't let out wire up here. Too many rocks and flotsam. You're most likely to snag a shopping cart or a Steve Flemmi girlfriend. You're not in Florida anymore, brother," Shark said with a sigh.

Peeler had not seen Shark wrestle with a decision like this since they took on the Conzalez gig the year before.

"I can see you're chewin' at your shoulder over this new gig. You know I always leave the decisions about where we go to you, including the jobs we take or pass on. It's always your call. But Skip, it's not like us to sit here hiding in the eelgrass. We're hunters, man."

Shark tilted his head to glance over to a boat three slips away as a woman jumped off the back of her boat with perfect form for her morning swim.

"I know, Peel. We have been loafing around and throwing the

lazy card from our deck onto the table. To be honest, the vacation has been nice, and needed by both of us, but I know what you're thinkin'. You're right, we gotta sketch out our next move. I know that the inertia bugs you and you get your usual ants in the pants, but kid, you plunged a friggin' gaffe into an international drug king's only niece. If I plotted us a southern course, we'd never make it past the gas dock in Atlantic City. Treasure the green grass, brother, and the fact that you're walking on it and not staring up at it."

Peel ran his fingers through his hair. Shark was always better at rolling out the big-picture chart and putting things in perspective.

"I know, Skip. You're right on a lotta fronts. It's just that we can't let barnacles grow on our hull."

"Here's the thing, Peel. At first glance, this appears to be an easy grab. Shit, this Jib guy acts like pulling an offshore swap is difficult. We know we can do 'em in our sleep. And although I've never worked with Canucks, I can only hope that they want to avoid staring at steel bars every morning as much as we do.

"If we're gonna do this, we gotta take into account what Jib said. This new shit that we're supposed to transfer is gonna be like kryptonite to these arm-pokers. They're not gonna be used to that first blast, and it sounds like many are only gonna show their faces at low tide. Blue and bloated."

Peel tossed a small rusted clamp into the calm marina water as he listened and processed.

"Skip, say we were to hang a shingle and open up a beach bar or something? I'd say one was badly needed at this painfully dull marina. Ya know, start serving drinks at eleven a.m. Plenty of bartenders looking to move some modest blow during shifts. Couple might even wanna whore, or at least broker where to find one? Then, all of a sudden we're local business owners and pillars of the community. We could donate to Adams-Graham Hospital and get our picture taken with the mayor at some charity ball. Skip, I ask you, is that more noble?"

Shark was taking his time and thinking about this from all sides.

"Yeah, Peel, I understand the hypocrisy on our part in what you're sayin'. Maybe we should make the run, grab our cut of the cash, and then shoot north? Spend the summer up in Maine—Bar Harbor, maybe? That wouldn't be a bad place to hole up in, find a quiet marina, count the booty, and stay outta sight.

Come Labor Day, we'll need to get out of these godforsaken northeast waters and head back to where we are comfortable, and have some contacts. We'll have a few bucks, and things should have died down by then."

Peel placed the old reel onto a milk crate and began sharpening a wire cutter.

"Well, Skip, maybe it's time to reach out to Justin? He found us before. Let's find him."

"Hey, Peel," said Shark, "did I ever tell you about getting hit by a baseball when I was a kid?"

"Nah, Skip," responded Peeler.

"It went like this. I was playing catcher behind the plate. Ya know, batting practice type of thing."

Peeler gazed at him vacantly.

Shark continued. "So this guy starts throwing meteors, I'm talking major fastballs. Whatever; I didn't pay much mind to the whole thing until one of our teammates stepped up to the plate. Like I said, batting practice."

Peeler looked at his boss now with a bit more interest.

"So the guy takes a strike. Then, again, he watches—strike number two."

Peeler's attention was waning.

"*Then*, on the third pitch, he clips a foul ball."

Shark suddenly became quiet.

After a few seconds, Peeler was frustrated. "Yeah, so what happened?"

Shark looked Peel in the eye. "The friggin' ball cracked me in the eye. I looked like I just got back from behind the woodshed. I forgot to wear a catcher's mask."

Peel was quiet for thirty seconds, then finally spoke.

"That sucks, Skip. Sorry to hear it, but what the hell does that have to do with us?"

Shark sat up straight. "Everything. It has *everything* to do with us. I learned an important lesson: Don't do stupid things. Very simple. Don't do dumb shit. Get it?"

"Clear as mud, Skip."

CHAPTER SIXTEEN

Crane Estate, Ipswich, Massachusetts

Puck McManus resembled a lizard. He had wide, reptilian eyes, cold shiny skin, and a tongue that would flicker in the air without warning, courtesy of a nervous tic he'd developed after serving as water boy for his high school football team. He made the unfortunate mistake of spilling Gatorade on the star quarterback's favorite game shoes, which had cost him an elbow to the retina. Since then, Puck had quietly slithered though the streets of the North Shore without detection.

Although Puck's drug peddler occupation was considered a plague on society, he fancied himself a mere entrepreneur capitalizing on a niche in the marketplace. Yeah, he'd heard the stories of local kids winding up in the hospital, most as guests in the ER, while a select few bought nonstop tickets to the morgue. However, he maintained a clear conscience. Puck had positioned himself as a caring businessman. One who gives back to the community. He envisioned his obituary one day listing him as a philanthropist.

As the fentanyl infusion used in heroin increased, the front-page stories of local tragedies had sadly become almost commonplace. Puck couldn't stand the thought of passively standing by and watching kids die. It was tearing families apart and ripping the fabric of the community. Most importantly, it was bad for business.

Puck stole a line from Dave Pirner and adopted the motto, *We'll create a cure. We made the disease.*

In addition to providing laced smack to local addicts, he conjured up a strategy for reducing customer attrition. He began to sell Narcan along with his usual stash.

This was a first for the region, a local drug dealer providing the same drug used by EMTs in overdose situations. Narcan was first approved in 1971 for use in blocking the effects of opioid overdose, and it was unusual to find it in the hands of the typical street dealer. However, the medical community had become porous over the years, and while certain drugs were supposed to be administered only by professionals, they were constantly finding new distribution channels on the street.

Guild Harbor would soon be flooded with festival partygoers, and while Puck badly needed to replenish his supply, he thought that Jib's latest plan for the exchange was odd. The fact that his middleman wanted to meet in Ipswich was strange, and the selection of a public venue where a big event was under way was more than a little unnerving. Lizards always prefer to remain surreptitious, under the cover of thick greenery.

The area was mostly known for the vast 2,100-acre Crane Estate; even the early settlers in the 1600s knew the property was a gem, deeming that the grounds *shall remayne unto the common use of the Towne forever.*

As he walked the impeccably maintained rolling lawn of the mansion, Puck's first thought was that there must be a wedding reception going on, given the noise level, which was strange for midweek. The estate was actually hosting the North Shore Business Association, where three hundred guests were reveling, networking, and engaging in various levels of extramarital flirtation.

Puck did as instructed and walked down the flowing expanse of land toward the ocean. He looked down at the handheld GPS, which displayed the exact coordinates of the rendezvous location. He soon found the large oak tree that had been selected for the handoff.

Puck didn't know much about big band music, but he found himself tapping along to the beat of a Buddy Rich disciple. He pulled out his cigarettes and tapped the pack along with the pounding of the distant drums. He lit up a Newport, leaned back against the tree, and waited. A check of his watch revealed that it was 8:59 p.m.

Suddenly, a figure dressed in black and wearing a mask appeared from around the next tree. Puck was startled, yet quickly focused. He was eager to vacate the premises before the party broke up for the night.

Jib's delivery mule approached and waved a soft hand at the air as a signal to keep quiet.

Puck ignored him and broke the silence.

"Thanks for being on time—this place is starting to give me the creeps. I told Jib I wanted three kilos. I know that's a large order for me, but between Guild Harbor and Newburyport, we got festivals and parties galore over the next few weeks," said Puck, whose defense instincts suddenly kicked in. "Hey, don't you talk?"

The courier looked around before presenting the plastic parcel to Puck.

While Puck found the black clothing and mask a bit over the top, the silent treatment seemed downright melodramatic.

"Okay, man. You keep quiet, then. Of course you won't mind if I taste the product? Don't think I don't trust ol' Jib—it's just that I don't trust who *he's* buying from, and you know, things slip by sometimes."

The courier made a "help yourself" hand motion.

Puck pulled out a Swiss Army knife and cut into the first brick-sized bundle. He stuck his finger into the slice, careful not to let any of the precious powder spill onto the grass. He touched his finger to his tongue.

He immediately tasted a sweet flavor. Too sweet. Puck's eyes went owl. "What the fuck is this?" he exclaimed, irate.

In a lightning motion, the courier dropped the parcel and rammed a stun gun into Puck's stomach. A blast of air soundlessly escaped his lungs as he folded up and fell back against the tree.

A few seconds later Puck felt the slight sting of a needle being stuck into his neck as his aggressor emptied a phenobarbital syringe into the already stunned dealer. Unable to move or speak, Puck maintained a trancelike, wide-eyed stare as he focused on the lights beaming from the mansion on top of the rolling hills which he'd found so captivating. He capitulated to the situation and immediately felt a sense of peace.

The courier began pulling apart thick tape from a spool and wrapped it around Puck, circling the tree four times in order to prevent him from slumping over or falling onto the ground. He remained quiet and stationary as the drug mule poured liquid all over every stitch of Puck's clothing, as well as the bottom few feet of the tree.

Puck experienced a scent that was sweet and invigorating. He then noticed the dark figure pull something out of a deep pocket. A second later he felt the weight of a lit Zippo lighter land on his lap. His clothes were burning, and then a rush of heat started to melt his lips and eyelids.

He tried to scream but couldn't find the breath. The last thing Puck saw in his now-shortened life was the mule running away, absorbed into the black night. Had any of the guests been out on the veranda stealing a smoke or a forbidden kiss, they would have smiled at the sight of the little bonfire, most likely set for a beer party.

CHAPTER SEVENTEEN

Guild Harbor Police Headquarters

Sergeant Anthony O'Doul was studying the *Boston Herald* with amusement. Howie Carr was belting away at some crooked state rep who'd gotten caught taking a land permit bribe, while the sports section boasted of yet another Sox victory on the road. Last night brought their streak to five.

It was setting up to be another usual day at headquarters, until Tony was interrupted by one of the new officers.

"Sergeant O'Doul, we're getting a lot of press inquiries about that incident in Ipswich."

"Whaddya mean?" said O'Doul as he took a slug of watery coffee. "What happened in Ipswich, and why do I care?"

Officer Deborah Quincy knew that O'Doul was old-school and snarky with the female officers. He still could not bring himself to view them as equals, even though for the last two years their collar rates had been significantly higher than those of their male counterparts.

"Some guy was set on fire at the Crane Estate. I mean, the whole shebang. Someone poured an accelerant, threw a lighter, and left the guy for embers."

"Shit," responded O'Doul. Rarely did anything faze the jaded sergeant. He pretended to only half give a damn. "Right on the estate grounds?"

"Yeah, Sarge. There was a function going on with a coupla hundred people, yet this happened without anyone noticing until the cleaning crew came in around midnight and smelled smoke."

O'Doul was a little shocked, and intrigued. The North Shore experienced its occasional violent crimes, but nothing this creative. Even to the hardened O'Doul, this sounded like an outright torture scene.

"They ID the victim?"

"Not yet," responded Quincy. "The crime lab crew is already trying to analyze the DNA, so hopefully we'll know sometime today. I would bet that it's somehow gang-related, although it's definitely a strange place and time to stage a hit."

O'Doul nodded. "Yet a perfect setting for a murder if you not only want the victim to be discovered, but also want to make some kind of statement, or spectacle. It's especially odd—"

He was interrupted by another officer who stuck his head through the sergeant's doorway.

"Hey, just to let you know, we received word that twenty yards away from last night's crime scene they found a stash of what at first appeared to be a heroin pouch. However, it turned out to be two kilos of powdered sugar. Maybe our killer's on the *Food Network?*"

While the others chuckled, O'Doul didn't. He was feeling heat that started on his shoulders and ran down his back.

Officer Quincy raised her chin. "I bet it's connected to that dealer who got iced in the alleyway a few nights ago. That sugar stash has to lead to a connection. It's way too coincidental."

O'Doul was nervous and unsure of what to do next. His immediate impulse was to get these damn meddlers out of his office, shut the door, and track down Jib Scola.

CHAPTER EIGHTEEN

Dunlap Neck, Guild Harbor

Amina put away the groceries that she had purchased earlier that morning when the supermarket first opened. She liked getting there before the retiree crowds began to aimlessly roam the aisles around nine o'clock. She also wanted to be early because the market was already going to be busier than usual due to folks stocking up for the festival.

As she was placing cans on a shelf in the pantry, she bumped her right forearm, already sore following an accidental burn the previous evening. She walked over to the sink and turned the cold water on full blast. Even with the sound of the faucet spilling into the sink, she heard the loud ring of Jib's cell phone.

After a few seconds, she could hear Jib's voice. He'd put the phone on speaker, so she could hear everything. O'Doul was on the line, talking *about* the Ipswich murder scene. Jib began yelling into the phone. Clearly the conversation was not going well.

Normally she stayed out of the captain's business, but she was curious as to what was transpiring. Jib rarely raised his voice at home, usually his oasis.

Amina opened the fridge and poured a tall glass of herbal iced tea that she kept handy for when Jib needed something soothing. While Jib appeared to be the consummate cool customer, Amina knew the other side of his personality, an alter ego plagued with tension and nerves. She put some crackers on a plate, placed it on a tray next to the tea, and headed toward Jib's office.

"Hey, Tony, I didn't light the friggin' guy on fire! Why ya calling me all shook up? What's the matter with you? Whatever freak show went on out there in Ipswich had nothing to do with us."

"They found more fake dope at the scene," said O'Doul. "I don't know what's going on, but someone's decided to start killing North Shore drug dealers, and it's people that we do business with! It's only a matter of time before your name starts getting tossed around, if it hasn't already."

Amina quietly entered the room and put the tray of refreshments on a table across from Jib's desk. She wanted her boss to see they were there but didn't want to interfere with the heated discussion.

"Thanks, Amina. Just leave it," barked Jib. "What happened to your arm?" he asked, noticing the burn.

"Oh, it's nothing. I got up in the middle of the night to heat up some milk, seeing as I couldn't sleep. I must have been half-dreaming, and bumped into the burner. Just an accident."

Jib shook his head and returned to his conversation.

O'Doul had barely taken a breath. "Jib, the sharks are swimming. The people who decide things around here are only going to put up with so much shit for so long. Buying your mansion is one thing, but human bonfires are not gonna fly. I know that you have visions of one last big score, but Jib, we gotta call it off."

If Jib could have strangled his partner through the phone, he would've.

"Tony, I may be breathing hard, but I'm maintaining my perspective on the situation. Listen, we're gonna retire and get out. We just need this one last shipment to put everything in place, man. Think about it. You can leave town with enough cash in your hands that you'll never have to look back. I told you about this Florida guy I'm hiring to facilitate our last run?"

"Are you sure this guy is gonna take the gig? I mean, all he has to do is listen to the hens cackling down on the dock. He could also just pick up a damned newspaper and he's gonna know he's buying a ticket to the dragon's lair. No way is this guy, if he's as savvy as you claim, gonna want the job. My guess is that he gets wind of the crazy shit going on around here and he'll be tossing his lines within the hour."

"Tony, just calm down and let's—"

"Sorry, Jib, I gotta go. Someone just stuck a note under my nose that says we're all expected for an emergency roll call in five minutes. I'll let you know what Louie and the rest of the brass are saying. Talk to ya later."

O'Doul hung up before Jib could respond.

Jib sat at his desk, sipping some tea as he pondered the situation.

Whoever had grown tired of Jib's success was obviously increasing the scope of their operating budget if they'd decided to start burning dealers on the estates of former tycoons. While the pressure was clearly getting to O'Doul, and Eel was not exactly showing his usual fervor for the work these days, Jib remained convinced that this last run *must* be executed. Captain Shark was just the man to pull it off.

Jib got up and paced the room, looking out at the harbor. His confusion was acute and his anxiety, well founded. He knew that in any successful operation, you had to set everyone up financially, and if you failed on that front, you had to kill them. There was no third option.

CHAPTER NINETEEN

Lake Tashmoo, Martha's Vineyard

The sun angled slightly north of the expected easterly glare that radiated from the bight into the land that thousands of years ago created scenic Lake Tashmoo on the northwest-facing side of Martha's Vineyard. Of course, Tashmoo was not really a lake filled with freshwater, fed by a mountain stream, but rather a natural slice in the terrain that allowed fresh ocean currents to quietly smooth their way in to chill the shallow, relatively still, and popular anchoring spot for pleasure cruisers and weekenders from the western side of Cape Cod.

Summers on the Vineyard used to mean beachfront barbecues and quaint window shopping—right up until President Bill Clinton's family and entourage had decided to make the Massachusetts vacation community their summer destination. Since then, the island had quickly evolved into an East Coast L.A., rivaled only by their island nemesis, Nantucket, already famous for mega yachts and naughty limericks.

A large, stately Cabo sportfishing vessel floated peacefully on an oversized anchor, the vessel's captain planning on spending a few days and hopefully not needing to reset position at three in the morning.

The vessel formerly named *Free Lance*—unfortunately, forced to abandon her old identity in pursuit of anonymity—had slowly cruised its way up the coast from the Georgia barrier islands over the past year. During the off-season, the fifty-foot Cabo would have stuck out like a shark in a swimming pool, but during the decadent Vineyard high season, this eye candy for boat lovers barely turned a head, which is just the way the captain liked it.

Former Boston attorney and assassin on the run, Justin McGee, poured another ounce of wax onto his already-pasty rag as he scrubbed a particularly stubborn spot on the port side of the helm station. He kicked up the level of elbow grease as he applied the second layer. He had always found this leisurely chore to be relaxing.

Justin and his unorthodox "family" blended right in with the summer throngs anchored in the calm Tashmoo waters. Marlene Dunn, Justin's soulmate, lover, and former target for a hired assassination, swam ten feet off of the Cabo's stern. Their quasi-adopted daughter, Michonne, called out to Marlene, asking which dive or jump she should perform next.

"Hey, Mom, this time, I'm gonna do a jackknife!" yelled Michonne, not waiting for a response. The newly turned twelve-year-old, glowing with excitement, grabbed one foot by the ankle and reached up with the opposite arm, causing only a little splash against the back of boat.

After a few seconds, Michonne surfaced and proudly boasted, "Mom, Justin! My jump was so good that my foot hit the sand!"

Justin knew that despite the outgoing tide, there was still plenty of depth for safe diving. He and Marlene had baptized Michonne into the smuggler's life one year ago, and now he just liked to keep things as calm as possible, letting her enjoy the chance to be a kid.

The little girl had happened upon Justin and Marlene's dock at the beginning of the most dangerous operation of their relatively short smuggling careers. Michonne not only had witnessed the dark side of their operations but had also been a prime mover in the violence necessary to ensure its success.

After a hellacious several hours of cleaning up the vessel and fleeing to the ocean in order to elude the authorities, Justin had connected with a contact in Jacksonville Harbor, who over the course of several hours had stripped the hull clean of all decorations and graphics, redesigning and renaming her *American Wake*.

After the new lettering and hull color had become a permanent part of the former *Free Lance*, Michonne wisely expressed her concern. "I heard that renaming your boat is bad luck. Is that true?"

"Well, honey," explained the seafaring assassin, "it's only bad luck if you decide to rename the boat 'cause you're tired of the name or disappointed with the boat. She just needed a makeover. Think about it—she's prettier and happier now, with fresh makeup and a handsome new ice-blue paint job on her hull."

The maritime facelift had been necessary to confuse any nautical authorities who decided that a random boarding was necessary. It also washed away the ghosts that still roamed a ship that had hosted more than one death.

Michonne rubbed her chin and smiled, satisfied by the explanation. "Well, okay. But what does *American Wake* mean?"

"Good question, sweetheart," Justin said. "It's a term used in Ireland for when an Irish citizen moves to America. His friends have a party for him just prior to his trip across the Atlantic. It's filled with optimism, but also carries that archetypal Irish warning against the unknown. It's a smart phrase, my dear, and one that will bring us luck wherever we go."

As the three regrouped now in the *Wake*'s cockpit, Justin wiped his hands with a clean rag as Marlene and Michonne dried off and warmed up with towels. Marlene fetched three bottles of water and leaned against the starboard padded fishing station, looking with a smile at Justin. She found him adorable, even with a splotch of boat wax smeared on his nose.

"Mom," said Michonne, "while we're still out on this anchor and not at the marina, can I take a hot shower below? My teeth are chattering."

"Of course," responded Marlene. "The fresh towels are in the usual spot in the starboard closet. Just yell if you need anything else, sweetie."

"Thanks, Mom," said Michonne as she disappeared into the vessel's salon, renovated and rebuilt after the damage incurred during the violence of a year ago.

With Michonne gone below and the prevailing westerlies light, Lake Tashmoo remained quiet as Justin and Marlene savored the tranquility. While Marlene enjoyed the quiet moments, she had grown to know Justin's every thought. She knew that something was weighing on his already heavy mind.

"Isn't it a beautiful day? The sun is out, the winds are fair, and the anchor is holding. Michonne is so happy. What could possibly be worrying you?"

Justin itched his left shoulder with his chin as he always did when he was steeped in concern.

"I got an e-mail, Marl."

Marlene's glance permeated Justin's Ray-Bans and shot down the back of his spine.

"Was it Darby? Be honest, Jus. Was it him?" said Marlene, her teeth clenched.

"No, Marl, no. Please, relax. Since our last encounter, we've been able to shake him. Put that whole situation in your wake."

"How can I? After what he tried to pull down in Georgia. That prick! I'd kill him this minute and run him through the bait grinder."

Everything came back to Marlene. It was only a year ago, when after chasing the lead all the way down the East Coast, the aging mobster had finally caught up with Justin, only to find him nestled in an out-of-the-way marina in Jekyll Island, Georgia.

Darby was amazed that he had found him at all, let alone the fact that Justin appeared to be hiding out with the assistant district attorney Darby had hired him to kill in Boston. And on top of that, it looked to Darby like the two of them had adopted a little girl.

Darby didn't care if they had opened a day-care center, he needed to take Justin, and take him alive. Normally, he would have shot him from a distance, but the FBI bounty for capturing Justin alive was too much to ignore. It was a unique opportunity for Darby, whose livelihood was evaporating around him with the implosion of the traditional New England criminal underground. Whitey was gone. The Angiulos were in jail, or dead. The Patriarcas were history. The Winter Hill Gang was defunct. The McLaughlins from Charlestown were all dead. The list was endless. It left few players at the table, and one was on the hunt for Justin McGee.

In retrospect, Darby should have kept to his normal methodologies and shot Justin with a long-range rifle from the marina parking lot. His goal of improving his proximity to the target required Darby to walk down the docks of Port Side Vow Marina, where strangers were welcomed like an Ebola virus strain.

While Darby didn't exactly scream *gangster*, his sweat-soaked cheap button-down shirt and matted hair did not exactly allow him to blend in with the Georgia coastal boating community.

It was Moe Miller who had stopped Darby on his way down the gangway.

"Hello, cousin. You appear to be lost," said Moe.

Darby snapped back, "Hey Jethro, outta my way. I ain't lost and I ain't your cousin, so you ain't gettin' a kiss. Go thump a Bible."

Normally, a confrontation with Darby McBride would have sent Miller to the hospital in a best-case scenario, but some of the other marina members overheard the tone of the greeting, and quickly hopped off of their boats to further Moe's point with this infiltrator.

The few seconds that it took Darby to attract attention and draw a small crowd caused enough of a stir that Justin turned his head. When his eyes met Darby's from afar, it turned his veins to ice. While most people would have panicked in such a situation, Justin acted on instinct. He quickly sent Michonne below and barked at Marlene to throw the lines.

Within seconds, the *Free Lance* was off the dock and moving toward the channel. As Justin increased his lean on the throttle, even while still in the no-wake zone, he looked back and saw Darby surrounded by a small mob. He chuckled to himself that if the marina members didn't break his jaw, then it was possible Darby would expire from a heart attack, knowing he'd just watched a million-dollar bounty calmly cruise away toward open sea.

Justin interrupted her thoughts.

"Go easy, Marl. We need to stay calm for Michonne. I received an e-mail today from Shark. He and Peeler are six hours north of here, hiding out in Guild Harbor."

Marlene's head dropped like a prizefighter capitulating to a worthier opponent.

"I would have sworn that Jekyll Island would have been the last we'd seen of them. Did that crazy Cuban drug guy ever catch up with them?" asked Marlene.

"Nah," said Justin. "I doubt he'd be sending me e-mails if he were dead and hanging from a highway overpass. I think they were smart to head north that day. The Conzalez family loses its eyes and ears the farther you get away from Miami, especially on a northerly route. They go radio-silent once you hit Atlantic City, where the New York element starts to kick in. Those goombahs don't take kindly to Cubanos sniffing around their territory without invitation. I *am* surprised to hear they're laying low in Guild Harbor, of all places. Beautiful town, but it definitely has its own share of others on the run from someone, or something. They'd be better off in Maine."

"Well, what did he *say?*" asked Marlene urgently.

"He wrote that he and Peeler are fine and have gone totally off the radar from anyone connected to the Florida rackets. That's the good news. The bad news is that since they've cut off contact with everyone in their Rolodex, the business opportunities have dried up. Sounds like they're livin' off a few bucks that they got from that small slice of Conzalez's salvage, but it's not enough to keep them on the lam for much longer."

Marlene looked skyward and let out a deep breath. "So where are you going with this? Get to the point. What's he suggesting?"

Justin calmly raised his hand to quell Marlene's simmering. "Honey, he has a business opportunity that fell in his lap in Guild Harbor. I have an old captain friend up there named Jib Scola. He's a contact from years ago, but we still trade correspondence once in a while. We somehow got on the topic of the increased smack trade between Guild Harbor and Nova Scotia, and I happened to mention Shark. I told Jib to seek him out if he's ever looking for a hand. I'm sure Shark wouldn't mind the payday.

"Jib asked me if Shark was someone who could be trusted, and you know, I vouched for Shark's abilities. That's it. It never entered my mind that somehow Jib, Shark, and I would ever cross paths."

Marlene shook her head. "You weave a tangled web, McGee. So what is Shark, or better yet, *you*, proposing we do? Remember, we're caring for a little girl now. We can't run off making drug runs. We still have enough of our funny-money stash from counterfeiting to get by. Plus, at some point we gotta figure out how to plant some kind of roots. You know, enroll Michonne in school and let her meet other kids and so on. What we have established is not exactly a normal life for a young girl."

"Marl, after all her little eyes have seen, can you envision her politely standing there sayin' the Pledge of Allegiance, or trying on a Girl Scout uniform and peddling Thin Mints? C'mon, Marl, this kid is too experienced to sit still and read Nancy Drew. And honestly, I think she's better off for it. Whether you like it or not, she's been indoctrinated into the *life*."

Marlene exhaled loudly and rubbed her fingers through her hair. "So, what do you propose, Captain?"

Justin donned his look of intense concentration. "Lemme e-mail Shark and tell him that we'll leave this rock at first light tomorrow. We'll plan on meeting him and Peel at some spot offshore, away from the fishing grounds and shipping lanes, where we can hear out his proposal firsthand and see what he's got in mind. We're gonna need money at some point, and if you truly want to find a place to settle for a while, the North Shore beats the hell out of the Vineyard. You'll be hanging yourself before the end of the first winter if you're stuck on this rock."

Marlene nodded, deep in thought, as Justin continued.

"The North Shore has some very nice communities with good schools, parks, plenty of kids. We need to hear the particulars direct from Shark's mouth about what they have cooking up there on Cape Ann, but it's something to consider. It could mean enough money—*legitimately printed* money—that we could use to rent a condo, buy a car, and just set up shop for a while."

Marlene was quiet for several seconds, and then burst out chuckling. "That would be funny, seeing you in line at Motor Vehicles, or at a supermarket deli counter, making sure your ham was *sliced thin*."

Justin smiled, relieved that the tension had eased somewhat.

"It sounds like a decent plan with a lot of potential. But there's one problem. Actually, maybe two," said Marlene.

"What's the snag, hon?" he asked.

Marlene grabbed his hands and looked directly into his eyes. "Jus, you're still on the FBI Ten Most Wanted List!"

Justin looked down. "I know, I know . . ."

"And one more thing," Marlene said, inhaling and breathing out. "I'm pregnant."

CHAPTER TWENTY

Antigonish Harbour, Nova Scotia

Captain Phineas MacLeod tapped his pipe against the faded wood that served as the summer home for his fifty-four-foot Wesmac custom fishing vessel. The cool, Canadian Maritime breeze soothed his skin and he tasted tobacco and salt as he inhaled. The remnants of early-morning fog and the slight drizzle added to the postcard-worthy setting at the old marina. He rubbed the thick, salt-crusted stubble on his weather-beaten face and for a brief moment, his busy mind rested and was devoid of thought. He then reached into his left vest pocket and pulled out a worn leather pouch that held today's supply of Captain Black.

As Finn packed the pipe he heard the crunch of tires as his cousin Bryce's pickup truck bounced from pothole to pothole in the marina's chomped-up parking lot. Finn appreciated Bryce's punctuality, and for a few seconds he reflected on how times had changed. Only five years ago he would've been waiting for Bryce to hurry up so they could go out and throw the lines in search of North Atlantic halibut. Opportunities had evolved since then.

The weary truck shuddered as Bryce threw it into park and killed the engine. The driver's-side door squealed as Bryce emerged, eager to sit down with Finn and plan their next cargo shipment for the Yanks down in Guild Harbor. Bryce's assistant got out and slammed the passenger door.

"Hey, Dogfish, can you grab some of that stuff to bring aboard?" barked Bryce.

"No problem."

Dogfish had worked for Bryce for over ten years. He was a friend and confidant, but most of all, he was a great worker. However, he had proven several times that he was a little dim in the dome.

While Bryce wasn't proud to be part of the growing Nova Scotia–New England drug trade, he needed the money to stay afloat, due to his financial commitments to a couple of ex-wives and four estranged children. While he missed the simplicity of life with Finn as part of a local fishing team, their catch of choice in recent years was certainly more lucrative.

Finn chuckled as he watched Bryce kick a half-dozen beer cans to the side as he walked across the lot, most likely left by some local St. Francis Xavier University students following a night of partying. The idyllic Nova Scotian seaside community provided the backdrop for one of the most prominent higher-learning institutions in Canada.

"Permission to come aboard, Captain," said Bryce, as he'd done hundreds of times over the years.

"Granted, as always," replied Finn. "You seem chipper on this rather dreary morning."

Bryce swung his leg over the starboard gunwale, careful not to slip on the moist deck.

"And why shouldn't I be bright-eyed, cousin? We're on the verge of what should be one of our bigger scores. Listen, I know you're still feeling guilty about making dope runs instead of dropping gill nets, but man, you can't beat the money. I'd be screwed if I had to rely on fishing to support my two broods. I wasn't as lucky as you, to have kept it in my pants and never settled down."

Finn laughed. "Bryce, you call your life *settling down?*"

"Well, maybe I did it with the installment plan. It was never consistent, but there were happy times sprinkled in among all the chaos." Bryce paused. "Hey, Finn, you okay with bringing Dogfish along with us for the trip south? That's a nice bird's nest we'll be keepin' warm. He's trustworthy."

"Yeah," Finn said. "Dog is solid, and we're gonna need him." Finn spat on the dock. "Thanks for being on time. Brief me on what we're lookin' at?"

Bryce pushed a buoy off of two lobster traps and took a seat.

"As I mentioned over the phone, I should have the new product delivered by tonight. It will take me no time to combine it with the usual heroin bundle and I'll wrap it up in one tight bale so it won't take up much space. The handoff should only take a minute or two. With Dogfish to assist with the lines and so forth, my goal is ninety seconds, maybe two minutes."

Finn nodded in satisfaction.

"The Yanks toss us the duffel full of cash and I send over the satchel of dope. Just like we've done a dozen times, only *this* time, we'll be giving them a new gift. Then, we bid farewell, spin the boat around, and head back northeast. Nobody's the wiser, and international trade among friendly nations continues to thrive." Bryce chuckled. "Most importantly, it will relieve me of another six months of money burdens."

Finn dragged on his pipe, deep in thought. He had become wiser over the years in that when it was time to make decisions, it was better to smoke than to speak too quickly.

After thirty seconds, he spoke. "Okay, so I get the gist of the whole transport part, but I don't understand this new drug, this sidio, or whatever you call it?"

"Tsulio, Finn," said Bryce, "It's called Tsulio."

"Fine, whatever. Call it fun dip, for all I care. What I'm getting at is why, if I'm Jib Scola sitting there down in Guild Harbor, why do I need *us* to procure a stash of Tsulio if it's made in the U.S.? Why not just get it stateside and save all of the time, expense, and hassle of dealing with a couple of Canucks? Doesn't make sense, Bryce. My gut is already getting acidic. Got any Tums?"

"I realize at first glance it makes no sense. Lemme explain. Do ya remember the Motherisk scandal a few years back?"

"Kinda. Sorta, yeah. Why?" asked Finn.

"Motherisk was a drug lab raking in thousands for performing drug tests across the five easterly provinces, including Nova Scotia. They were highly respected and ran a profitable business, using testing methods that relied mostly on hair samples. This went on for several years until it was uncovered that the testing methods were shoddy, and subsequently the test results proved bogus. This affected hundreds of drug cases, including child custody disputes."

"Lovely. Yeah, now I remember."

"Lotta decent people, and not just *guys*, lost access to their kids," said Bryce. "Canada, at her finest moment. There was a woman in Toronto who was convicted of feeding her toddler son a near-fatal dose of cocaine, and the charges were all based on results from tests conducted by Motherisk. The results were ultimately deemed inaccurate, so to cut to the chase, in 2014 the woman's conviction was overturned and the ruling affected the fates of hundreds, if not thousands, of pending and past drug-related cases."

Finn nodded. "Yeah, that was a media shit-show."

"Well," continued Bryce, "a couple of years earlier, the same thing happened down in Massachusetts, where a senior lab tester was caught performing bogus drug tests. She not only wound up in the clink, but her actions rippled throughout the entire New England legal system, resulting in thousands of drug cases getting tossed."

"Okay, I appreciate the history lesson, but you're not answering my question. Why does Scola's Cape Ann drug op rely on a coupla Canadians to get its supply of this new dope?"

"Simple," responded Bryce. "There's a ton of pressure on the US drug overseers to keep Tsulio in the hands of qualified medical professionals. I mean, it's a major concern down there due to the rampant opioid crisis. The US FDA has taken a lot of heat for approving Tsulio to be used for nonmilitary applications, for which it was designed in the first place. You know, it was just supposed to be administered to wounded soldiers in Iraq and shit like that. The FDA is making it almost impossible for nonmedical types to get their hands on the drug, 'cause it would be a political nightmare.

"Our Canadian government drug regulators, for now, anyway, don't face the same public pressure the US FDA is facing, and as a result, the drug transfer between pharmaceutical producers and wholesalers is a bit more lax. Again, for *now*."

"So, what's our window of opportunity?" Finn asked. "I mean, how long do we have until our guys up here crack down harder on distribution?"

Bryce shrugged. "Who knows? Like anything else, it will go unnoticed until the media can connect an increase in overdoses with illegal wholesaling of Tsulio. Six months? A year, if we get lucky, and the bureaucrats stay lazy and fed."

"So," said Finn, "we're getting the shit from one of your Canadian contacts easier than Scola can get it down in the U.S., even though the damn drug is made in America?"

"That's right. Again, that's accurate for *now*. It won't be forever, which is why I want to make this run a good one, 'cause there probably won't be many more that will contain this new junk."

"Okay . . . That's a lot to digest. What's our move in the short term provided, you get the Tsulio ASAP?"

"Well, you talk to Jib later this afternoon and tell him we're right on schedule, and could probably meet his transfer boat off the Maine coast whenever he wants."

Finn was quiet for ten seconds while watching a gull screech by.

"All right, man. I'll tell him." He rubbed his forehead. "I wish I shared your level of excitement, but I guess I see your point. This run *is* a unique opportunity. I'll top off the fuel tanks today." Finn stared at the water, as he often did when in deep thought. "I'll ring Jib before dinner. I just need time to think about strategy, and take all of this in."

Bryce smiled. "It'll be a quick and easy exchange. Like trading marbles."

CHAPTER TWENTY-ONE

Jeffries Ledge, Fifteen Miles East of Cape Ann

The *American Wake* bobbed up and down in the gentle one-foot swells off the coast of Rockport, Massachusetts, as Justin awaited the arrival of his former smuggling partners, Shark and Peeler.

The tide was slack and devoid of any obvious current, and Justin felt no need to throw the anchor. Luckily, the sea conditions had been close to perfect during the ride up from Martha's Vineyard, so everyone on board was relaxed.

Michonne was busy belowdecks working on a jigsaw puzzle, while Marlene and Justin were sitting on deck chairs in the cockpit.

"I can't believe we're going to have a baby, Marl. It's still not real."

Justin McGee had been uncharacteristically quiet since hearing the news that he was to become a father. Most who knew Justin would never picture him in a paternal role.

"Shhh . . ." Marlene put her fingers to her lips. "Let's just keep it quiet for now. I'm sure Michonne will be excited, but I don't want to tell her just yet. Let's see what craziness is in store for us after meeting up with Shark and Peel."

"I know, you're right," responded Justin. "It's just that I never thought, never *dreamed*, of being a dad. I've been so damned self-centered my whole life, I don't know how I'll do. How I'll function."

"I don't think there's a Bill Belichick playbook for parenthood. Most people just figure it out as they go along."

"Yeah, but Marlene, our situation is especially unorthodox. You know the TV show *How I Met Your Mother?* What am I going to do? Have the kid watch *How I Tried to Murder Your Mother?*"

Marlene sported half a smile. "Nobody in their right mind would have expected me to ever forgive you, much less welcome you into my life. Nobody is ever going to understand, nor should we expect them to. Ours is a world never to be understood by outsiders. But Michonne is adjusting to this upbringing, and I'm certain that our child will as well."

Justin shuddered, "Stop talking about it. It's too much right now."

Marlene retorted, "Right *now*, it's too much? Jus, it will always be too much for you. But you'll adapt."

"Honey, I've spent most of my adult life in the role of a destroyer. A taker. Shit, at my core, I'm an annihilator. I've never been a nurturer. In the past, I've never cared for anyone but myself."

"Jus, you're a selfish bastard, for sure," Marlene said with a chuckle. "But you're selling yourself short. Aside from trying to blow my head off, you have been a perfect gentleman, and you've made Michonne happy."

Justin smiled tentatively.

"Plus, Jus, think of it. Had you not been such a great mentor to Michonne and taught her the way around a sniper rifle, I would be dead right now, back in Georgia, at the hand of that dirtbag, Shred. Because of you, Michonne had the knowledge and courage to fire the shot that saved my life. Probably the lives of Shark and Peeler as well. Hon, we're a different breed that the world will never understand. Our kids might grow up without the white picket fence and Saturday-afternoon playdates, but they'll be strong, street-smart, and loved."

"Speaking of which, Marl, are we going to find out the baby's gender?"

"At some point. First I need to get a medical exam, whenever we can get off this damned boat."

"Soon, Marl, soon," said Jus as he rubbed his hands through his hair. "Shark should be here shortly. There's a good hospital in Guild Harbor."

The next few minutes passed quietly with the exception of the gentle lapping of the ocean against the hull of *American Wake*.

Michonne kept busy down below while Justin scanned the westward horizon. After several more minutes, a boat appeared at the edge of Justin's sight.

"Hey, Marl, I think I see them. There's nobody else around, and that looks like the outline of the *Booty Call.*"

"Okay. I'm going down below to check on Michonne. I assume she'll keep busy for a bit while we talk up on deck. Who knows what's on Shark's mind?"

With Marlene below, Justin readied for the *Booty Call's* arrival. He set two fenders over the starboard side of the cockpit, and with his handheld marine radio, hailed Captain Shark.

"Hey, Shark, I can tell it's you. Lookin' good at a nice cruisin' speed. Tie 'er up to my starboard."

Shark responded immediately. "Roger that. Thanks for making the trip, Jus."

"My pleasure. I knew our paths would cross at some point."

Shark made a semicircle with his vessel so that his port side would snug up to the *American Wake.* As Peeler worked to make the lines fast so the boats were secure, Shark hopped over into Justin's cockpit. The two smuggling partners exchanged bear hugs and shoulder slaps.

"You look great, Shark," said Justin as he stepped back, "and you too, Peeler!" he yelled over to Shark's first mate.

"Thanks, Jus. It's been a long time," said Shark. "Being on the run is not nearly as fun or exciting as it is in the movies. I hope Peel and I made the right decision to head north, but I knew we had to get outta Conzalez's backyard."

"Any sign that he's on to you?" asked Justin.

"Nah. But our luck won't last forever. We killed his *niece*, after all!"

Peeler climbed over onto the *American Wake* about the same time Marlene emerged from below. The four were now officially reunited, and more hugs and pleasantries were exchanged.

Justin had set out four deck chairs, and Marlene brought up some refreshments from the galley. Peeler eagerly grabbed a Corona, while Shark opted for a Pellegrino.

"Hey, Marl," asked Shark, "where's that wonder girl of yours?"

Marlene smiled. "She's down below working on a puzzle. I'll bring her up in a few, but I wanted us to be able to talk openly. You wouldn't have reached out to us and called for an offshore meeting if there wasn't something significant on the table."

"True," said Shark. "Here's the story . . ."

For the next ten minutes Shark relayed the entire chain of events that had led them to this offshore rendezvous. He told them about his visit with Jib Scola, and how he was entertaining an offer for a smuggling run that could have eyes on it from the start, and thus the game required some extra players.

Shark also talked about the cargo that was to be snagged, which contained a new drug, and how it was initially designed for military use, but how it would inevitably fall into the wrong hands on the street. This is where Jib Scola hoped to take down a score by overseeing the maiden shipment into Guild Harbor.

Justin spoke up. "So, Scola wants to outsource the grab. I get that. But why don't you and Peeler just go out, do the gig, and grab the payday. Why involve Marl and I?"

Shark rubbed his chin. "I'll be up front Justin. This job is spooky. I'm already a marked man up and down the Eastern Seaboard because of a friggin' drug czar. And I'm trying to run a high-risk operation in waters totally unknown to me. If shit suddenly goes ugly, I got nowhere to hide and nobody to turn to. I want you guys along for brains and security. I envision your sniper rifle to be my lifeline if things go awry. Basically, you'd be playing the role formerly played by Gerbil, but hopefully with a little more poise."

Justin slowly shook his head. "Gerbil . . . Man, that poor bastard. Not a *bad* guy. You know, he was just kind of a bull in the china shop of life."

The group was silent for a moment until Marlene spoke.

"Shark, what's my role? I gotta make plans for somebody to watch Michonne while we're gone. I'm not taking her into another smugglers' gun battle ever again."

Shark responded, "We'll work out that piece. Jib won't be coming with us, so I'm guessing I can get him and his housekeeper to look after Michonne."

"Shark," said Justin, "I know that Scola and I have connections from way back, but I can't vouch for who he is, or what he's become. I gotta trust your instincts on this one, as you and Peel agreed to take this assignment."

"My gut says that he's all right to deal with this one time. I gotta believe he wants out of the business and is gonna vacate Guild Harbor with a stash of cash that will let him disappear down in the islands somewhere. I think his intentions are pure on this one. Hopefully, the Canadians are of the same mind-set.

"It's a big deal," continued Shark. "This Scola guy has a lotta eyes on him, and the heat is intensifying. I hope he realizes that if he successfully lands this gig without a hitch or a gunshot, then it's time for him to count both his blessings and his money and get outta Guild Harbor."

Marlene, who had been quiet, spoke up. "So, Shark, when does this all go down?"

"Our plan is to leave the dock tomorrow night around six," Shark said. "I wanna hit this run hard and get it over with. Y'all have mine and Peeler's cells."

Justin leaned back in thought. This was an opportunity he did not want to squander, but he suddenly had another vision of the strategy.

After Shark was out of earshot, Justin turned to Marlene. "Babe, this could be a good score. But I wanna do it another way."

Marlene wasn't shocked that Justin was looking at this from all angles. His eyes were a bubbling Jacuzzi. She was curious as to what he was cooking up.

He looked at the sky as if grabbing an idea from the night air. "Marl, I don't think I want to leave Michonne dry-docked for this one."

Marlene didn't know if she should entertain Justin's fancy, or if she should stab him right there and then. Would be an easy temple entry.

CHAPTER TWENTY-TWO

Guild Harbor, Office of the Mayor

"Thanks, Travis. Please send her in," said Mayor Trish Hine into the speakerphone on her desk. She brushed aside the papers strewn in front of her and awaited her guest.

Trish looked around her office to make sure that nothing looked messy or out of place. She was very particular about appearances. She believed in the concept of *Everything speaks* that her mother had taught her years ago. Trish knew she had plenty of critics in the old New England city. There still existed voter blocks that would never warm up to the idea of a female leading a city dominated by a masculine heritage.

When the police captain entered, Mayor Hine greeted her warmly.

"Good afternoon, Captain Washington. It's kind of you to meet with me on such short notice."

"Oh, please, Madame Mayor, I prefer when you call me Louie. I'm not one for formality."

The mayor smiled. "Louie it is, and to keep things even, I'm still Trish."

The two shook hands and took seats across a small coffee table on the other side of the room. The mayor always conducted her meetings in one of two places. If she liked and respected her guest, which was certainly the case with Louie, she preferred the simple, comfortable coffee-table arrangement.

87

However, if she was meeting with a foe and wanted to establish dominance, as was the case with certain local union leaders, Trish preferred to sit behind her large, oaken desk, seating her guest in a deliberately low seat across from her.

"Do you take coffee, Louie?" asked the mayor.

"Oh, no thanks. I knock it off by mid-morning, or else I'm all jitters."

The two women poured themselves glasses of lightly sweetened lemonade, and Trish smiled as she looked around the room, and then at Louie.

"Imagine this city fifty years ago. You know, full of sea dogs and wharf rats. Rough. Betcha none of them ever would have envisioned that the mayor and the police captain would be women. A black and a Jew, no less."

"Yeah," chuckled Louie. "Times have certainly changed. I actually don't know a lot about my family history. My mom died when we kids were young, and my dad was toiling away up here in GH, heading offshore chasin' fish. He wasn't around much, so I never got a chance to hear many stories about my family's history. One of my brothers in his senior year in high school did a project tracing our roots, and he claims that some of our ancestors were actually slaves back in the day. Supposedly they moved to the New England coast after the Civil War and took up carpentry and fishing. I'm not sure how much of that is true. All I know is that my daddy worked like a dog so that his kids could get an education and hopefully have some semblance of a better life. Unfortunately he died young, so he never got to see what we accomplished."

Trish asked, "Was he in a fishing boat accident? There are way too many stories like that in this town—all over the North Shore, for that matter."

"Nah, he died by accident, but not while fishing," responded Louie, who then suddenly changed the subject. "So Trish, what about your background? Did you get to learn much about your heritage growing up?"

"I did, fortunately. I'm not sure if that's good or bad. Most of my family fled Germany during or after the Holocaust. Fortunately, my parents got out safely and I was born in Boston, but some of my ancestors didn't fare so well." Trish leaned back in her chair a bit and took a deep breath. "My aunt and cousin were rounded up and placed in a concentration camp."

"Oh, God," whispered Louie.

"Yeah, it was a scene beyond nightmares. The way the family story goes is that my aunt's camp was visited by the SS general Otto Ohlendorf sometime during the war," The mayor paused. "Have you ever heard of the *Einsatzgruppe D*?"

"No, I haven't," replied Louie.

"Well, it was the Nazi unit under Ohlendorf's command. Historical accounts report that they alone killed ninety thousand Jews during the war, and my aunt and her baby daughter were among the victims."

Louie said, "I can't imagine . . ."

"Nobody can!" exclaimed Trish. "It gets better. My aunt and her daughter were slaughtered rather late in the war when Germany was on its heels and supplies were running low. Ohlendorf ordered his butchers to have my aunt hold her baby up close to her chest. Of course, this was after my aunt was raped several times by several SS.

"Their killer fired one shot that penetrated both of their hearts instantly. Why use two bullets, when one will suffice?"

Louie was speechless.

Trish brushed her right hand at the air. "Ah, forget about it for now. I could go on, but we have other matters at hand. Not least of which is the question of why some local vigilante has all of a sudden decided to start murdering our most illustrious street drug peddlers? And killing them in a most ghastly way, as you know."

"Many citizens are saying it's some type of Bernie Goetz who appears to be cleaning up the community."

"Well, be that as it may, we can't have lawlessness in a city coming up on its busiest time of year. Summer is crucial for our economy, and everyone in Guild Harbor needs to feel safe. Even the filthy bastard drug dealers. I won't tolerate some rogue who has decided to take the law into his own hands."

"Trish, my officers and I are fully aware of what's happening. Please trust that we're doing everything in our power to get the prick that's doing this. We just need time. I'm not going to use this as a complaint session about being understaffed for the upcoming summer season, but the reality is, we just don't have the resources to scour every inch of the city, especially during events like the festival, which is just around the corner."

The mayor nodded. "I understand that you might be taking my comments as an insinuation that you and the department are not performing at a satisfactory level, but please don't look at it that way. I'm your biggest fan, Louie—and more than anyone, I know that to be a woman holding positions like ours, in a city like Guild Harbor—well, it means that we have to do our job better and more efficiently than the good ol' boys. You can trust that I have your back."

Louie nodded, with a look of gratitude.

"We just need *some* kind of progress, and ideally, we need to have an arrest made before the festival. There's nobody else I'd have more faith in than you to get the job done."

Louie placed her hands together. "Thanks, Trish. That means a lot, coming from you. I know we could share some anecdotes over a glass of wine on what it's like to be a professional woman working in what is basically a men's locker room. Thank you. We're on it. I, one hundred percent, want this guy caught before the festival weekend."

Trish nodded in approval.

Louie continued. "While we're talking about serious matters, did you have a chance to review my classified e-mail on what could be coming around the bend? I'm not trying to overcomplicate things, but if this new pain medication called Tsulio winds up on our streets this summer, it will make the fentanyl-laced smack look like baby aspirin."

"I read what you sent, and I'll admit, it's frightening," said the mayor, in a tone of genuine concern. "You know that I lost my nephew to an OD on fentanyl-laced heroin a couple of years ago. My sister will never be the same."

"I'm sure that, for your sister, her son dies again every day," said Louie.

The mayor was quiet before responding.

"Louie, if this Tsulio is as strong as you say it is, then we could have nothing short of a mass atrocity on our hands if the local dealers get their mitts on it. From what I've read, this stuff is military-grade; doesn't that mean it will be safeguarded like a virgin's flower?"

"I'm not sure," Louie said. "The formal FDA announcement last November touched on all of the safeguards that would be in place to prevent street access to Tsulio. But c'mon, that's what the drug makers at Purdue said about OxyContin. Call me a cynic, but if there's money to be made on the street by building a better mousetrap—in the form of a more-potent opioid—it's gonna get in the wrong hands, and it's not gonna take long."

"All right, Captain, how do we know when it's infiltrated Guild Harbor? I mean, I'm certain the local dealers are not going to take out an ad promoting a grand opening sale. How will we know?"

"Unfortunately, Trish, we're gonna find out the way we always do when a new street drug is unleashed. We're gonna see the number of zombies explode at the Adams-Graham ER, or we're gonna start finding bodies like the one that washed up in Folly Cove. That's the only real telltale."

Trish was briefly quiet before responding.

"You e-mailed me that this shit is ten *times* more powerful than fentanyl?"

"Yeah. And as far as I know, the only people in town who are playing for the home team who know about this stuff are you, me, and my police chief downtown."

"I was gonna ask, Louie—what does Chief Olson think about all this? The dead dealers, the upcoming summer throngs, the arrival of a nasty new poison? Does he have his head around this?"

"May I speak off the record, Madam Mayor?"

"Of course."

"The chief is aware of what Tsulio is and what it could potentially do to our community. But, to be frank, he's thrown the whole thing into my lap. This project is my responsibility. I'm the head of the soon-to-be-formed task force.

"To be blunt, Trish, he's not a bad guy, but he's knee-deep in his plans to run for that upcoming congressional seat being vacated by the retiring Peter Trough. You've probably heard the rumors? Trough is resigning in anticipation of the indictments coming down following the missing federal money from the Route 128 widening project between Danvers and Guild Harbor. His fingerprints are everywhere on that one, and he's gettin' out of Dodge while he can.

"Meanwhile, our ever-ambitious police chief thinks he can squeeze just a little more pulp out of his political contacts on the North Shore to make a run for Trough's seat. What I'm getting at is that I'm on my own on this one, and I can't solicit support from my peers until I have just cause to believe that Tsulio is on the street."

The mayor was quiet.

"Well, Louie, I'm here to help with anything I can do from the standpoint of my office, but between a murder epidemic, a new opiate coming to town, and a boss with stars in his eyes, I don't wanna hand you a bag full of unpinned grenades."

Louie inhaled deeply. "Yeah, Trish. That's about the size of it. And to make matters worse, I'm still dealing with a segment of the population who, under the guise of social media, promulgates the contention that Guild Harbor never had a drug problem until a black woman was placed in charge of overseeing the narcotics side of public safety. Gotta love those tweets you read at three in the morning when you can't sleep."

Mayor Hine nodded. "I hear you. Believe me, folks have written a few tweets about me, too." She sat back in her chair. "Please keep your eyes open with the whole potential Tsulio epidemic, and regarding our vigilante—I think I can bump up your budget another fifteen percent or so, especially in light of the upcoming festival. We have some unallocated money that came in for marketing and promotion of the town, and I can't think of a better way to use it. Just talk to my assistant Travis as you leave, and he'll lay out the logistics to get the money under your control for the department. There won't be any of the usual delays or red tape."

Louie gave her first genuinely happy smile of the day.

"Thanks, Trish. I won't let you down. Maybe after we catch this bastard who's hunting dealers, we can have that chat over a glass of wine, at a joint nicer than Kelsey's?"

"You got it, Louie," said Trish. "Keep me posted. And if you run into any bureaucratic nonsense, ignore the normal protocol of communication channels and just fire me a text."

Both of the women stood, shook hands, and exchanged shoulder pats.

"Louie," said Trish, "if this Tsulio does hit the streets, what are the odds that maybe it actually *won't* be the scourge that we fear? Any chance we can beat it?"

Louie rubbed her chin.

"Think of it this way: It's Final Jeopardy, the category is *Presidential History*, and your opponent is Doris Kearns Goodwin."

In silence, Louie walked out of the mayor's office, in equal parts invigorated and petrified.

CHAPTER TWENTY-THREE

Justin on the Street

To stay alive in his profession for so long, Justin had to know the value of information. After he situated *American Wake* and made sure that Marlene and Michonne were comfortable, his gut told him it was time for a little reconnaissance. And that meant going into town and finding a potential gem of a source: a police officer, alone, walking his beat.

Didn't take long.

Justin put his gun to the head of the beat cop.

"What's your name, Officer—and I mean your street name?"

"They call me S-S-Sway," the cop stuttered. "R-really, man. You're g-gonna shoot my ass? Do you know what will happen to you if you pull some shit like that in this town?"

"No," responded Justin. "But, I *do* know what will happen to *you!*"

The cop quickly realized Justin had experience with such situations. This was not just some street punk.

Justin continued. "Listen, Sway, I don't wanna shoot anyone. All I want is information. So spill, or be spilled."

"Whaddya wanna know?"

Justin stepped back to give the guy some space. "Relax, man," he said. "How are the drugs getting into Guild Harbor, and how do I queer their flow?"

"You're asking me how to stop the *flow*? No way! There are bad dudes involved. Lotta money. People been getting offed around here lately. You read the papers?"

Justin's shoulders relaxed. He knew this guy would give up something; he just had to remain intimidating and keep up the pressure.

"Sway, I gotta ask—are you brand new? I mean, like I just found you under a Christmas tree? I don't care who you are. I don't care who your family is, or how they'll mourn your passing. I'm happy to introduce you to your favorite drainage ditch this very night. Do you understand? I need information. And I *will* kill you. No hesitation."

The beat cop responded, "Man, do your worst, but I ain't no snitch."

"I admire loyalty," said Justin, as he paced within a twenty-yard radius, "but loyalty will sometimes get you killed. That's your name now. *The Loyalist.* Do you like your new name, Sway?"

"Screw your mother!" said the cop.

"Okay," said Justin. "I get it. Resilient. Small-town tough guy. Big badge in a small backyard. Hmm . . . You see, I have some money. Money is good, as you know. Buys a lotta shit. Make your best lady happy. Right, Sway?"

"D'a fuck you getting at?"-

Justin took a deep breath.

Sway shifted toward his port side.

"Currency buys shit, Sway. But all you cops know that. Just takes a little coaxing. Might buy your old lady a washer and dryer, right?"

Sway remained a statue.

"So, here's how it's gonna go," said Justin. "You are gonna give me every bit of information that you have. Drugs coming in. Drugs going out. The beauty is that then you'll be a free man. Give me what I want, and then you walk."

Sway looked left. Peered to the right. Finally, with a movement of his eyes, Justin could tell that the street cop was contemplating his proposal.

"If you don't cooperate—if you don't run with my bulls—actually, Sway, if you annoy me in the slightest way, my nine-millimeter and I will play piñata with your thick-headed skull."

Justin stayed calm. Sway did not.

"O-okay, okay! Whaddya wanna know?" said the young cop.

"Information," responded Justin. "Nothing more, man."

"All right," said Sway, "all right. Just cut the threatening shit."

"That's fair," said Justin, holding the gun in a less-menacing manner. "Now, spill."

Sway stared at the wall and then started talking.

"There's a lotta drug shit going down. It involves a guy named Scola and other people you might have heard of. There's a lot of H coming into town, but it ain't close to pure. All fentanyl these days, and it's killing people—and not just the users."

"It's that bad of a plague?" Justin asked. "Someone's even killing the locusts who are moving the shit from barroom to alley?"

Sway felt more comfortable now that Jus looked satisfied with his response. Almost like it was an affirmation. He was finally a bit more optimistic that maybe Justin wasn't going to kill him.

"It's a disaster, man, and it's not just Guild Harbor. It's all over New England, and beyond. And it's showing no signs of slowing down. There are rumors that it could get even worse."

Justin turned his head.

"Shit, Sway. Not sure how we're going to beat it. Shit . . . I'm sorry you were so forthcoming."

"Whaddya mean? I was just being honest. What's going on? You look weird."

Justin gripped the cop by the arm.

"Hey, man, you're a good dude, and I appreciate the information. But now, you're a witness and a liability."

Sway's eyes bulged, "No. Please, no!"

"Nah, Sway, relax. You caught me on a forgiving day," said Justin. "But now I know who you are and I can see your badge number. Hopefully you'll show some gratitude and pretend that this by-chance meeting never happened."

"Of c-c-course. Whatever you say. Just please don't kill me."

"Nah. Quite the opposite," said Justin, as he handed the guy a C-note.

"Th-thanks," said Sway.

"I do have one more question that I expect to be answered. If it seems that there is some indication the players in this nasty trade are known to the community, why hasn't more action been taken?"

Sway took a deep breath out of gratitude that the Reaper was going to move along to other projects.

"Two reasons," responded Sway. "One is that there ain't enough proof to take a hard, legal approach. And with these cases, the DA's office only gets one shot. If they blow it, it's a cluster-F."

"And?" asked Jus, who was pretty sure he already knew the second reason.

"Well, there's a lot of talk that there could be some pretty powerful locals involved. Again, no proof, but it's rumored to be the type of people who could ruin your life."

"That's usually the case, Sway," said Justin.

Sway was grateful he was going to live, but he knew he wasn't going to end up totally unscathed.

"Unfortunately," said Justin. "I can't just walk away and have you phone the precinct."

He pistol-whipped the officer just hard enough to let him sleep for bit, hopefully waking up with just a little fog, and a long life still ahead. Justin reasoned that he was not going to be in town long enough to be recognized. Plus, he thought that maybe his impending fatherhood could be softening him.

CHAPTER TWENTY-FOUR

Home of Jib Scola, Dunlap Neck

Jib paced the floor of his study in anticipation of Jasmine's call. He picked up his cell as soon as it rang. He had memorized her number, as he hadn't dared to enter Jasmine's name in his cell even under an alias.

"Hi, Jasmine," he said curtly.

"Hello, Mr. Scola."

"Remember—call me Jib."

"Oh yes, right," replied Jasmine. "Well, Jib, I've been working on your case. You were wise to suspect this Tsulio drug could become a major problem."

Jib was silent.

The chemist continued. "I did the research. The chemical construction is unlike anything we've seen, even with the strongest of opiates. You're noble to want to research how it's going affect your community."

"Yeah," said Jib, "just trying to get the facts and do the right thing."

"Well, you are definitely in the right to be concerned," said Jasmine.

Jib audibly inhaled.

"Bottom line. The effects of Tsulio on Guild Harbor will make the '91 No-Name Storm look like a butterfly breeze."

Jib rubbed his facial stubble.

Jasmine continued. "You see, it's basically Economics 101. It's a better product, and will be remarkably inexpensive once it finds a consistent trade channel. It will be impossible for the dealers to not beg, borrow, steal, *and* kill in order to get it. It's synthetic, and will open up a whole new market. It will be virtually impossible to put this genie back in the bottle."

"Unreal . . ." said Jib, who was in awe for reasons totally unknown to the chemist.

"The other problem is that while the drug takes effect in seconds, it's not going to last long," said Jasmine. "That's dangerous, because an addict will want more, and fast. Could be a complete disaster, to put it in mild terms."

Jib was quiet for several seconds.

"Thank you, Jasmine. I will wire payment to you immediately."

"Thanks for the project, Jib. I learned a lot—most of it nasty. But unfortunately, as a chemist, I'm used to a lot of bad news, especially when looking into this kind of product."

"I bet," said Jib. "Thank you for your work."

"You're doing a good thing, looking into this time bomb. Have a good evening, Jib."

Jib rolled his head from side to side, sat staring straight ahead.

He heard the doorbell chime, and then Amina's footsteps as she walked to the entryway and opened the large oak door.

"Good evening, Captain Shark. It's a pleasure to see you again," said the always gracious Amina.

"Evening, ma'am. I believe Jib's expecting me."

"He is, Captain. I'm sure you remember the way, but allow me to escort you."

As Amina led Shark down the hallway toward the back of the residence where Scola conducted all business matters, he couldn't help but marvel at Jib's collection of "curiosities" which seemed to blanket all available wall space.

"Hey, Amina," said Shark, "bet y'all could have one helluva yard sale."

Amina looked back and smiled.

"Yes, I think we could, Captain. The North Shore is loaded with wealthy collectors of rare pieces. I'm sure that we'd have a bidding war on our lawn." She pointed toward the door of the study. "Please go right in. He's waiting for you."

Scola stood behind his desk, and as usual, was deep in thought as he gazed across the wide reaches of the old New England harbor.

Shark crossed the room, and as the two men of the sea shook

hands, Shark looked out the window in an effort to share the same vision that seemed to have momentarily transfixed Jib.

"I'm sure you appreciate the view, Captain Shark," said Jib. "The anecdotes all around us would be the envy of best-selling novelists and Harvard historians alike. History that's been written by brave bastards over the years, and that's still being written today. The fishermen here are hearty, Shark. Damn hearty. Regardless of how the government tries to quell their efforts, they still plug along while keeping tradition alive. People might guess that I love this house because of its fancy address and design, but the real reason is because every window is its own telescope across the harbor, allowing a look into the secrets of this city. And I get to take it in every day."

Jib found Shark's eyes.

"Where's your colleague tonight?"

"He's around. I requested that he keep an eye on the vessel, if he doesn't pass out from the rum first," Shark replied. "As I mentioned on the phone, we appreciate your offer for the assignment, and we take it seriously. I don't want anyone near my boat until the mission is done."

Scola paused.

"Smart move. And thanks again for accepting my offer. When I hadn't heard from you, I thought maybe your interest level had waned."

"Nah. I just wanted to consult with our mutual friend, Justin."

Jib nodded. "So, McGee will be a part of this outing. That should certainly increase the intensity. May I ask what his role will be?"

"No, Jib, you may not. When a man at his level is in play, I want control of all facets of his involvement. Just know that he supports the mission and is comfortable with my being in your employ. Plus, the less information floating out there, the better. And don't worry, I'll pay him out of my cut."

Scola put his hand in the air as if to calm the moment. "Shark, he's all yours. Perhaps I can regroup with him once everything is buttoned up?"

"Whatever you wanna do," said Shark.

He noticed the many built-in bookcases that appeared to house old hardcovers.

"Impressive library, Jib."

"Yeah, well, even us Guild Harbor fishermen can appreciate a good read," said Jib with a smile.

Shark grinned, then said, "We leave in twenty-four hours. The plan is to meet your Nova Scotians thirty miles east of Portland Harbor, so you'd better get on the horn and get them moving. Fortunately, the marine forecast calls for fair conditions, but they'll be shooting across a lotta open water."

Scola nodded. "Indeed. I'll ring 'em shortly. The cash that you will be transporting is ready and will be delivered to your boat fifteen minutes prior to your departure by one of my guys. He'll be disguised as a cast fisherman who's hanging around the docks. Nobody will be the wiser as to what he's carrying in his sea bag."

"You don't seem like a man who fools around or takes unnecessary risks," said Shark, feeling reassured. "I like that, *and* I like the fact that you're in agreement this is to be a *one-time* assignment for me and Peeler. I'll deliver on my end, and I want my cut of the take without incident. Then, I'll be throwing my lines. Don't plan on ever seein' me again."

"That's the plan, Cap'n. We're on the same page," said Jib. "Now, if you'll excuse me, I need to tend to some logistics. I wanna ensure that your vision comes to fruition without any unforeseen obstacles."

"Thanks, Jib. I'll show myself out. I'll expect your cash mule at my boat as planned."

CHAPTER TWENTY-FIVE

Adams-Graham Hospital, Guild Harbor

Eve Coven faked sick and was in the process of banging out early from her shift in the ICU in Guild Harbor's Adams-Graham Hospital. The fifteen-year veteran was well-liked—so much so that the on-site pharmacist never asked any questions when she needed a little extra whack for her weekly grab.

The druggist was involved in Nurse Coven's small and selective drug ring, which was part of one of the city's most surreptitious opiate operations.

Nurse Coven had learned how to grease the rails. After all, she was overseeing a side business that was multilayered, and sufficiently unknown to the Guild Harbor constabulary.

Her recently deceased father, a lifelong Guild Harbor machinist and marine mechanic, had finally let his liver explode three years ago. His bequest to his daughter was a valuable, commercially zoned machine shop that had not yet been sold and developed into a real estate office or a web design firm. For anyone who cared, this was due to the continued "mourning" by the owner's grieving daughter.

Coven had gutted the basement of the shop and turned it into the only clandestine, invitation-only swingers club on Boston's North Shore. Walking into the main floor of the property conjured up images of an episode of *This Old House.*

But if one ventured down to the basement, they would find an after-hours club that would immediately remind a Vegas swing-joint czar of the Studio 54 days.

Coven was smart and kept her clientele intimate, quiet, and free of fear of being exposed. Her guests included local politicians, community leaders, and, most importantly, hospital executives who grew bored of the North Shore winter shortly after the New Year's revel.

Granted, she had to work to establish the support of the local medical community in order to find glorified drones to write the ED and opiate scripts, but eventually most of them showed up at the club out of boredom with their occupations, wives, and lives. It didn't matter to Coven. Once in the door, she didn't care if you professed to be a surgeon or a sturgeon. All the money was crumpled and green.

In the end, by providing a venue for sexual services, Coven was provided with inside access, which simply meant that if she needed to leave early on some random afternoon due to her migraine issue, she would undoubtedly be in possession of any and all things that began with "Oxy."

On this day Coven left the hospital quickly and headed to the parking lot. She was scheduled to meet another intermediary in ten minutes, and she didn't want to be late.

Everyone knew that Jib Scola controlled the distribution infrastructure, but Coven had another outlet that evening. She had been told by a client that there was a guy who would take her load at a ten percent premium if she could meet him at a quiet place where the transaction would be quick and clean.

"To hell with Jib Scola," Eve whispered to herself. "His time has come and gone. Prick is gonna get pinched."

Coven walked through the maze of cars in the lot, fumbling for her keys as she reached her car. "Damn!" she said as she dropped them on the ground. She realized her nerves were starting to perk.

She finally managed to open the door and place the contraband on the floor in the back, on the passenger side.

Coven fired up the engine, looking left and right as she'd been taught in driver's ed, back in the day. She threw the car in reverse and drove to the nearby exit, which would put her on a dark road heading out of the Adams-Graham Hospital grounds.

She was driving down the shadowed, leafy road when she suddenly felt a strange motion coming from the front right side of her car.

At first it was a lopping noise, which quickly became the screech of a flat tire.

"Dammit!" she cursed. "I don't have time for this shit!"

Eve liked to talk to herself.

She pulled over to the right side of the road and steered the car into a bank of tall wild grass and weeds. She sat still and contemplated her options.

While she was thinking, two hands reached over from the backseat and made fast a wire garrote around Coven's neck. As she tried to fight, she realized that the more she resisted, the deeper the wire dug.

Her last thoughts were not shock that she was being murdered. That was a foregone conclusion. The surprise stemmed from the size of the hands that were wrapped in long, black gloves.

After a short struggle, she rested her right arm over the gear shift of the car and was at peace for the first time in years. Maybe for the first time, period.

CHAPTER TWENTY-SIX

The American Wake

Justin threw down a suicide king which Michonne had called wild before their hand of seven-card open.

"That'll teach ya! Right back to school, my dear. Full house!" Justin raised his hands in victory.

"Dad, that's not cool. You're not playing fair, and you're taking advantage of a little girl!" Michonne said with a crooked eye.

Michonne knew that her adopted dad never gave any quarter when it came to poker. He rarely did, for anything. He yearned for his daughter to be tough and independent on all levels.

"Sorry, hon, but *you* called what was wild, and it came back to bite you. I'll take the pot, thank you very much."

With that, Justin reached across the table and hauled back a hefty stash of wooden poker chips. They didn't represent any monetary value, yet their currency was reflected in the father-daughter memories.

The two were enjoying some quiet competitive time together while Marlene was lying down belowdecks. The persistent waves of nausea were becoming debilitating, and she craved rest and a few consistent hours of sleep.

This gave Justin the opportunity to engage in some heartfelt conversation with his little girl.

"Honey, you're strong and brave, and I'm proud of you. Mom and I love you, but we don't exactly live a *normal* lifestyle that's considered typical for little kids."

Michonne flipped a few pieces of hair over her right ear.

"Let's face it, Dad—I am *not* a typical girl, and I'm never gonna be. I don't wanna play soccer. I don't want to be on a phone all day, texting. I love the life that you and Mom have given me. I feel strong. So, I've been through a lot, but you've given me the closest thing to real love that I've ever had. Now, what's on your mind?"

Justin was taken aback. He placed his cards on the table and took a sip of his water bottle.

"Well, I know that I've taught you certain skills. Actually, you came to us with skills that you learned on your own. But I helped you perfect them. *And* you saved Mom's life on that horrible day last year."

Michonne blinked twice. She looked proud, but like she wanted Justin to get to the point.

"Michonne, I might need to ask you to help me again. It will also mean that you're helping Uncle Shark, too. It's something that I've been thinking about, something I haven't shared with Mom because she's sick and I don't wanna upset her."

"Dad, I'd do anything to help you and Uncle Shark. Tell me what you want."

"Well, ya see, I have an opportunity to make some money with Uncle Shark. I know that we don't talk much about all that stuff, but it's what keeps us going. Mom's gonna be outta things for a while, so I'm looking to you to fill in on a key assignment."

"Whatever you need. I want to do whatever I can to help you and Mom, to make us a strong family. I know Mom isn't feeling well because I'm going to have a little brother or sister. I overheard you talking about it, and I'm happy."

Justin smiled and squeezed her arm.

"Okay. We have an assignment tomorrow with Uncle Shark. It's *really* important, and it's going to help the three of us. It's also going to help Uncle Shark, but he just doesn't know it yet."

Michonne looked confused. "Okay, I guess. Why don't you include Uncle Shark in what you're thinking?"

" 'Cause, sometimes, honey, you just gotta keep your cards close to your vest. Just like a poker game."

Michonne chuckled, "Okay, Dad. What exactly do you want me to do?"

Justin was so proud of how strong Michonne had become.

Firing on all cylinders, beyond her years.

"Well, remember how you saved Mom's life by shooting at that bad man who was going to hurt her? I'm sure that wasn't easy for you."

Michonne just looked into Justin's eyes as he continued.

"I might have to ask you to do a really hard assignment like that again. If you don't want to do it, it's no problem at all. I can make other arrangements. I shouldn't even be asking you to do this. But I guess I can't help but be curious, to see if you're interested."

"Dad. You're asking me to do what you taught me, and yes, I want the assignment. I am your daughter and we are a family. A *different* kind of family, but a family all the same."

The narcissistic side of Justin caught a glimpse of the child he had created. A perfect little girl. A highly intelligent poker player. A loving daughter.

"Hopefully you won't have to do *anything*. I just want you to be prepared in case something goes down where we need to step in and help Uncle Shark. I hope our involvement is minimal. This is really Shark's assignment, but I owe him big-time for that fiasco last year in Georgia. I know I should be disgusted at the thought of bringing my daughter on a dangerous mission, but honestly, you've got the most talent of any of us right now," Justin said. "I'm afraid that I've grown a bit rusty."

Michonne touched his hand. "Dad, it's no problem. I'm not afraid."

Justin breathed out his nose. "Like I said, you've grown into a strong young woman. Your skills would be the envy of a battlefield general. My time is ending. Not my time on this Earth, but my time in *the life*."

Michonne gazed at Justin with a curious stare.

"My business is a young person's game. I've done it for a long time and I've done it pretty well. But my mind and body are telling me that it's time to focus on you, Mom, and the new baby. I've taught you the skills. As much as it would seem twisted to outsiders, if they heard me say this, I want you to assume my role within our family."

Michonne nodded slowly.

"In order to be a survivor in our world, and in our business, you need focus. It requires *extreme* concentration, and my aging mind isn't up to that level anymore. And that's dangerous. It's lack of drive and direction that could get us all killed. You, however, have youth and determination on your side. If you think that you're ready, then I want to officially pass my duties on to you. This mostly includes protecting your mom and the new baby. I can still handle taking care of myself, so don't worry about me. I just need to step back a little. How do you feel about all of this, honey?"

"I feel strong, Dad. I feel strong and *alive*. Of course, I'll always protect our family, and that includes you. I wanna take on your duties."

Justin leaned over and kissed her forehead.

"I want you to be safe, Michonne. Please be careful. Be sharp, fast, and quiet. Always remember that *silence* is your greatest weapon."

Michonne smiled.

CHAPTER TWENTY-SEVEN

Late-Night Phone Call

"Yeah, Justin, what's up?" said Shark groggily. He had already gone to sleep for the night.

"Shark, I wanna hash out our plan for tomorrow night. My thought is that you and Peeler take *Booty Call* to make the swap. The way I look at it, the most dangerous part of this mission will commence as soon as you reenter the harbor and try to get the shit on land safely, without interference from anyone who might be curious."

Shark rolled over and grunted. "I'm listening."

"Me and Michonne will be the only two aboard *American Wake*, and we'll make visual contact with you as soon as you get within the breakwater."

"Marlene is smart to sit this one out, being pregnant and all."

"Yeah, she's all kinds of sick right now. I can't bring her along. At this point, she'd be a liability. I'm gettin' her a room at that new hotel downtown where she can rest. Hopefully, Michonne and I are just going to observe the operation from a distance. Ya know, watch you cruise through the harbor, dump Peeler off at the dock with the shit, and then get the hell outta there. Trust me—I don't want this to end up being a shit-show with my daughter on board."

Shark was quiet on the other end.

"I know what you're thinking—it sounds insane—but she's the strongest backup I have right now. It's not like we can advertise online for a consultant for the evening. I don't want her in danger, and I don't think that's gonna happen. Again, we're just providing support for this gig. It's like carrying a gun for protection. You love having it, but hope you never have to use it."

Shark let several seconds pass before responding.

"All right, Jus, it's your kid. She's an ace shot. Knowing that she's on board the support vessel will give me extra incentive to stay focused. Sounds like we have a deal."

"Good," Justin said.

"Sounds like we're not in Kansas anymore. This could get dicey. What are the other pieces to your plan?"

Justin offered a rough layout of the mission. Even though both men were seasoned players and knew that even the best-laid plans never turned out quite as expected, it was crucial they have a clear understanding of how things were supposed to transpire.

"Okay, let's do it," said Shark. "We're going to hell anyway."

"Save me a seat," Justin said.

CHAPTER TWENTY-EIGHT

Home of Jib Scola

Amina was always afraid to eavesdrop on Jib, but she couldn't keep herself from listening in on this heated call—especially since he always used the speakerphone.

"Wait! Whaddya mean you're doing the pickup alone? Are you out of your mind?!"

"Jib, it's the best way. Just me and Peel, as it's always been. We shoot up the coast, toss the cash, grab the dope, and then steam home."

"You're going up there alone with that zombie of a first mate? With all *my* money at stake! What happened with getting the help from McGee?"

Amina couldn't wait to report this exchange to her partner.

"Jib, you obviously trust these Canucks. We're good. Peel and I have a proven record that we can handle any situation. Peacefully or otherwise."

"This was not on the friggin' menu!"

Shark calmly responded, "Jib, the real danger to the mission occurs once we get back into Guild Harbor. That's where anyone, whether it be law enforcement or otherwise, takes their claw swipe. Justin will be there to have our back upon delivery. With his daughter."

Jib exploded. "His fucking *what?!* His *daughter!* Wait . . . wait. This whole thing has gone off the rails."

"Shark, how old is his daughter? Shit! What is this, 'Bring Your Daughter to Work Day' for assassins? Are you people are out of your

111

fucking minds?!"

"No," Shark said calmly, trying to defuse the conversation. "We will get this done."

Amina's mind raced. Jib was clearly on edge, and she needed to reach out to her partner right away. While she was ashamed of her betrayal, she knew that her operation benefited the higher good.

As Jib continued to rant on the phone in the next room, Amina slowly crept up the back stairwell to her quarters, where she could find some privacy. She punched in the digits of a phone number known to only three people in the world: Amina, the recipient, and whoever doled out cell numbers at Verizon.

The phone rang seven times before a voice came on at the other end.

"Whaddya got, Amina?"

The maid felt trepidation about giving her report, as the stakes were high, but she knew this was no time for hesitation.

"Well, looks like we need to move faster than anticipated. Jib and his crew are planning to execute soon. The rendezvous with the Canadians plus the trip back will take several hours, but it doesn't seem like they're gonna wait too long. Sounds like a slim crew is gonna make the run. However, there's gonna be backup once they return to Guild Harbor."

The voice on the other end paused in thought.

"That means that I need to work fast. Is there *any* way you can delay their departure? You know, buy us a coupla days?"

"Nah, they're rollin'. I think while this is Jib's charter, the helm has been turned over, whether it's voluntarily or not, to his hired guns. I met these guys, and while they don't seem *that* intimidating at first glance, from what I overhear, they have a *résumé*."

The other voice interrupted.

"So do I, Amina. So do I. I'll die by falling into the lobster pound, or I'll take a slug in the temple. I stopped giving a damn a long time ago. This Tsulio shit is gonna attack our town. If it means dead drug dealers, so be it. It beats kids falling off of jetties, too zonked to realize that even while stoned, gravity still applies."

Amina gathered her thoughts. "Okay. Just let me know how I can help."

"You've helped more than enough. I'll keep you posted, but I think at this point, it's up to me. And me only."

CHAPTER TWENTY-NINE

Guild Harbor Waterfront

The screech of the boat lines being tightened around the pilings—they stretch with rising humidity—told Captain Mary-Louise Washington that summer was fast approaching.

Summer's antics made for a chaotic time for the Guild Harbor PD, even worse for Louie, whose department chief was a mental no-show. Louie was the best at what she did and earned the respect that came with it, but from May through September, the whole squad needed leadership.

Visions of the approaching season played out in Louie's mind as she took a bite of her turkey wrap. She was tired of waiting for her invited guests to arrive.

Two seagulls had fixed themselves on a bench next to the oversized picnic table where she was eating. They stared at her, hoping she'd toss them a piece of the sandwich. Louie lurched forward with a hand motion to shoo them away. However, seagulls in a New England tourist town do not scare easily. They view humans as sucker meal tickets instead of threats.

She heard a din of voices behind her and guessed it was the sound of her lunch dates.

As the three men approached, they knew to take their seats on the other side of the table so as not to invade Louie's personal space.

The trio consisted of three of Guild Harbor's most well-known low-level drug dealers. They had worked with Louie before as an intelligence pump.

One might think it odd that she knew of their activities and didn't arrest them, but these three were relatively harmless, basically just dealing weed to tourists who were looking to get high and enjoy a day on the beach. They were more valuable as active informants than they would be sitting in a minimum-security jail learning how to make pottery.

The so-called leader of the group was Chico Main, and he'd brought along his colleagues, the Risotto brothers, Peter and Paul.

"Good afternoon, Captain Washington," said Chico as the three sat down.

Louie stuffed what was left of her sandwich into a paper bag and tossed it into the barrel six feet away.

"Nice shot," said Chico. "Two points for the captain."

"Save your praise, Chico," Louie said as she wiped her hands. "I appreciate your coming on such short notice."

While the park was unusually empty at the moment, there was still a chance they could be noticed by locals. Many would think it strange that the local police captain was sitting out in the open with three known hoods, but this was Guild Harbor; the rest of the world's rules didn't apply. And besides, those who knew Louie would realize that whatever she was up to, there must be a good reason for it.

"So there must be something big goin' down for you to summon all three of us," said Paul Risotto.

"There's somethin' that's lit," said Louie. "I don't have to review for you what's been happenin' to some of your peers over the past coupla weeks. It seems that Guild Harbor has a sort of vigilante on its hands, and whoever this guy is, he feels he's cleaning up the town by killing off drug peddlers. Local *merchants,* like yourselves."

The Risottos exchanged looks while Chico responded, "Yeah, we get what's been goin' down. How could we not? It's messed up, 'cause whoever this guy is, he's not playing softball. I'm no detective, but he's obviously making some kind of statement. I mean, that shit over in Ipswich? The crazy bastard tied a dude to a tree and set him on fire. That's nuts, man!"

Louie nodded. "Yes, indeed. As the old saying goes, fellas, *This ain't no sippin' tea.* I would imagine with all the violence, you three clowns are looking over your shoulders twenty-four, seven?"

Peter Risotto finally spoke. "Nah, Captain. As you know, our crew just peddles a little weed here and there to tourists. We're no different than all those gift shop owners downtown."

Louie laughed. "You guys kill me. You're comparing yourselves to the local merchants sellin' flip-flops? Shit, what's next? You gonna join the *Chamber of Commerce*?"

Chico smiled. "Not a bad idea, Captain. I hear they can get you a health plan."

The three hoods chuckled.

"Well, in light of everything, you might just need one, boys," said Louie.

"Not the way we see it, Captain," said Peter. "The guys getting offed are all high-level dudes. Running smack and pills and shit. You know we don't touch that stuff. Who the hell is gonna take out three small-timers like us?"

Louie nodded. "You're probably right. But anyone who's crazy enough to light someone on fire just might want to pick you three off for sport. Target practice, perhaps?"

"We'll take our chances, Captain," said Chico. "Figure if we watch each other's backs, we'll be all right. We act as lookouts when the situation calls for it. Other than that, we just go about our business and look forward to the season. Ya know, it's been a long winter and we could use the money."

Louie swiped the crumbs from the table. "Let's pretend I didn't hear that. Anyway, I gathered you here because I need information, and I expect you to give me what you have. Even though I agree that your operation is rinky-dink—which by the way is why I don't throw cuffs on you—you've lived here all your lives. You've got your ears to the street, and you've proven valuable at times."

"Rock on," said Peter Risotto.

Louie got to the point. "What do you know about this new wonder drug called Tsulio? I know you got wind about it before little ol' me. What's the chance of it coming to Guild Harbor, and when? Who's gonna import it, and how are they gonna get it here?"

Peter Risotto spoke up. "You're gonna be disappointed, 'cause we don't know much."

The three nodded their heads in unison.

"Captain," said Chico, "that shit is military-grade. Yeah, we know the FDA approved it and shit, but from what we hear, that stuff is strictly for high-level medical use and is under strict lock and key. No way it's gonna hit the street."

Paul Risotto chimed in. "Plus, Captain, that shit would be bad for business. I don't know the particulars, but it's supposed to make fentanyl look like Flintstone vitamins, so why would dealers want to put it out on the street? They'd just be killing off their own customers. We might be low-level players and not the brightest bulbs, but we understand economics."

"Tough to keep a disco open if you keep killing the dancers," said Peter.

"Yeah, Captain. It'd be like opening a deli downtown only to serve poisoned food to our patrons. We'd be outta business in a week. Makes no sense for anyone. Bad move."

Louie sat back in thought. "You know, you guys never cease to amaze me. Yeah, you understand the lack of incentive for a *logical* smack dealer to start cutting with Tsulio, but gentlemen, let's be real. If there's money to be made, guys are gonna move it. These smack movers know that if a client dies, they'll find three more within a day. They don't look at the big picture. I mean, shit, half of them are jacked on their own product. Like any other addict, their personal drug first and foremost is *money*, and most of those guys just think about the short-term fix."

The three dealers were quiet.

"So," Louie continued, "I've gathered you here 'cause I want to know who's got the connections to get the product and who has the ability to bring it to Guild Harbor."

Chico exchanged glances with the Risottos, and then responded.

"Captain, I don't think I'm talkin' outta school here. We all know the only guy with the brains and connections to get his hands on hard-core shit like Tsulio is Jib Scola. I mean, I'm not rattin' the guy out, but come on—he's not exactly hiding his newfound wealth."

Louie nodded. "You're not telling me anything I don't already know. We've tried to put the snips on Jib and build a case, but so far, he's been too good, too smart, and too careful. His lifestyle is not helping his cause long term, and we'll get him eventually. The problem is that the damn DA's office won't pounce unless it's an ironclad collar. As of now, he's been just slippery enough to stay outta the crosshairs. He's smart. He's not violent, and he doesn't screw anyone outta money. Dare

I say, he's a straight shooter when it comes to drug runners and keeps his operation at a moderate level in the grand scheme. Jib is not exactly Tony Montana."

Peter responded, "Yeah, but Captain, everyone knows he's got someone in your department who's got his back. Any idea who it is?"

Louie shot back, "No, but if I did, I wouldn't tell you three stooges. Anyway, Jib's set himself up pretty tight, but he's gonna step in dog shit one of these days, and you better believe I'll be the first one to clamp the cuffs on him. Matter of time, guys." Louie's glare got hotter. "You're certain that he's the *only* player who could get his mitts on Tsulio?"

Chico paused before saying, "Yeah, Captain. He'd be the guy. As you know, he uses his maritime connections to bring in product. He's got coastal connections in every port from here to Halifax. I'd say the delivery would be the ol' *Two if by sea.*"

Louie slowly nodded.

"Okay, gentlemen, if you want to stay in my good graces, do me a favor and keep your eyes and ears open, and don't stray too far from town over the next couple of days. Consider yourselves under *unofficial* house arrest, and Guild Harbor is your home. It's not like you three have much wanderlust. I want you on the lookout for information regarding Tsulio. Are we in agreement?"

The three hoods nodded eagerly as Louie gave them the usual warning at the end of their meetings: "Keep your operation two-bit. Don't try and go Miami on me and diversify your product base. If you ever try and escalate your operation, you'll find yourselves hog-tied in a holding cell the same day. I got so much shit on all three of you that the D.A. will buy me flowers. Everyone on the same page?"

Chico spoke for the group. "Of course, Captain. We're just local guys making a simple living. We don't need mansions on Dunlap Neck."

"That's good to hear, Chico." Louie smiled. "Like the song says, *I love you just the way you are . . .*"

CHAPTER THIRTY

Booty Call

The exhaust fumes that wafted through the air could not kill the early-summer smell of low tide off the Cape Ann coast as *Booty Call* rounded the Twin Lights and headed northeast toward the rendezvous point with the Nova Scotians.

With Shark at the helm, Peeler focused on making sure all the lines were set that would be required to rendezvous port to port with the Canadian vessel. Even though it was early in the trip, the monotony of busywork quelled the usual anxiety that Peeler felt during an operation.

They were now steaming full throttle with a course set for the roughly three-hour run east of Portland, Maine. The vessel was deceptively fast despite its appearance.

Shark was quiet. This was supposed to be a quick smash-and-grab assignment. Now it involved a new component in the form of an especially precious cargo. Not to mention the fact that his backup sniper upon returning to Guild Harbor would be a young girl. He found it funny that while her peers were waving pom-poms, Michonne would be wielding a Barrett M82 sniper kit with an effective firing range of almost twenty football fields.

In Shark's opinion, Justin was a good man. Solid and trustworthy. But this mission had taken on a new light with the addition of his adopted daughter. In the end, it was Justin's kid and his call, but in Shark's mind, they had moved from playing the slots to the baccarat table.

"Hey, Skip," said Peeler, "enough of the cloak and dagger. What's our plan? This is supposed to be an easy pickup from a coupla Canadians, right?"

Shark looked at the boat's steady wake, rubbed his forehead, and turned toward his first mate.

"Peel, what we're planning to *import* to the Guild Harbor is a plague. We may as well spray the whole town with Agent Orange. But we need the money, and the shit is going to get there anyway. Like the Red Sox yelled out in 2004, *Why not us?*"

Peeler shrugged his shoulder as if to shake off a bug.

"Hey, Skip. What if these Canucks realize how valuable their cargo is and decide to take our money, give us *two in the hat*, and then go broker the stash with some connection in Portland?"

"Relax, Peeler." Shark couldn't help but agree with Peel's fears but couldn't let on.

"Scola's dealt with these guys for four or five years. They're businessmen. They want the score, and they're not overly greedy. They're also smarter than the rogues we had to deal with down south. They know to stay reliable. That's how the cash remains steady, and nobody gets hurt, or worse, pinched by the Coast Guard."

"You're the boss, Skip," responded Peeler as he returned to negotiating the lines.

Two hours had passed when the voice of Captain Phineas MacLeod invaded the radio with the predetermined code names for their respective vessels, referring to the vessels' hailing ports.

"*Ann*, this is *Francis*. Come in, Captain."

Shark grabbed the receiver.

"Yeah, *Francis*, this is *Ann*. I have you on radar about four miles to our northwest at three-oh-five on the compass. Request permission to proceed as planned."

Because of Mother Nature's magnetic variation, if *Booty Call*'s compass read 305 degrees, it meant the Canadian vessel was really at 290 degrees. Shark tweaked the wheel in order to establish a beeline.

The radio fell silent, Shark knowing that the lack of chatter meant all was in place.

Peeler spoke up. "Skip, we've got contact. What's our next move?"

"We wait, Peel," responded Shark. "We wait, and never appear overanxious. The impression to give is one of apathy. Shit, we've got nothing but time. Our board of directors meeting was canceled," chuckled Shark. "It's like playing poker. You never dip your hand, and never fidget in your chair."

Peeler nodded. Not for the first time, he admired Shark's grace under pressure. That's why he was captain.

After a few minutes, the two vessels were close enough to gain visuals.

Captain Finn approached at a five-knot speed. He also had the luxury of calm seas and fair winds out of the west, all of which were perfect for a portside tie-up.

Shark yelled back, "Okay, Peel. He's swimming like a spring swan. Just what we want. I'm gonna put the bow into his port stern, and you make us fast."

"Aye, Skip," assured the first mate.

The two vessels met and Peeler immediately went to work, as did Bryce on the Canadian vessel. The time for radio contact was over, and Shark decided to address the Canadian captain old-school.

"*Francis*, thank you for rendezvousing with the vessel *Ann*. I trust that your trip was favorable. I know that we have some important cargo, so with all due respect, I'd like to suspend formalities and move right along to keep things smooth."

Captain Finn chuckled to himself. The more the American talked about taking things nice and easy, the clearer it became that Captain Shark was nervous. Finn always marveled at how transparent the Yanks were.

"Vessel *Ann*," Finn called over, "while we're not exactly transporting *Little Boy* over the Pacific, I do agree that we carry unique cargo. It looks like our mates have made our vessels fast. I think you have a duffel bag for me?"

Shark's quick breaths tightened his chest. His stress increased with every calm word from the Canadian.

"Aye, Captain," responded Shark, who then yelled to his first mate, "Peel, throw the bag."

Finn lit a pipe which almost made Peeler jump overboard. For some reason, the first mate was spooked about this mission more than usual.

Peeler tossed the sack across the rails into Bryce's hands.

Shark watched and immediately yelled over to the Canadian, "Okay, Skipper. You have what you need. Now it's time for international trade to commence," he said, maintaining his composure.

"NAFTA at its best!" Shark then yelled to Peel, "Put your catcher's mitt on!"

Bryce went down below and then returned with a duffel bag of roughly equal size. He shouted over to Peeler, "Here she comes, Yank!" as he tossed the contraband over *Booty Call*'s bow.

Peeler caught it with Jerry Rice skills and quickly headed toward the stern of the boat in order to bury the parcel belowdecks.

Shark marveled at how small the package was compared to the value of what was hopefully inside, which reminded him.

"Hey, Peeler! Look inside that damn thing! Make sure we have what we're looking for. If you open it and it's about to explode, please let me know," he added with a nervous laugh.

Peeler took the bag below and unzipped it. As he opened it, he marveled at what was inside. It was a bunch of taped bricks and white packages. He was not a drug expert, but this was not a bundle of herring bait.

"Skip, I think we gotta take a leap of faith on this one. Looks like the real thing."

Shark seemed satisfied. He was dying to head south.

"Thank you, Captain," he yelled to Finn. "Peeler will release the lines. Safe travels back north."

To which Finn replied, "You too, Skipper. Glad this exchange was uneventful. Make sure you remind Scola that if anything, I'm consistent."

Shark yelled back, "I'm sure he'll appreciate the good news."

Peeler emerged from below and let loose the lines that bound the two vessels. Within seconds they were free to proceed.

Shark tapped his horn to announce his exit and then plugged in a waypoint back to Cape Ann.

CHAPTER THIRTY-ONE

Lynn Classical High School, June 1984-

Louie Washington always sat in the front of the class and was never too shy to speak up to engage her instructors. Some of the other students thought of her as a boaster who liked to show off her intellect, but in reality, Louie just loved to question and learn. She loved every crumb of knowledge she was able to acquire. While most of the other students viewed their time in school as tedious, for Louie, it was a gift, something that was shared every day for nine months of the year. If anything, it got her away from the chaos that she called home.

She was relishing her AP History class as her instructor, Mr. Richards, quizzed his students in preparation for the final exam, coming up in two weeks.

"Can anyone tell me, *as measured by population percentage*, what was the deadliest war ever fought on American soil?" asked the thirty-year teaching veteran.

The class was silent. Although Louie knew the answer, she hesitated. She was self-conscious about her ability to memorize everything that she read. She sometimes took flak from the other students if she raised her hand too often.

After several seconds, a boy in the back of the room raised his hand. Mr. Richards immediately pointed to him. "Ah . . . I *think* it was the American Civil War," he said.

"Great answer, Pete. And frankly, that's always the most popular response. It makes sense, as the Civil War, in terms of *numbers* of the population, was definitely the deadliest war ever fought in America.

However, in terms of *percentage* of the population killed, that answer would be incorrect. Good try, though. Anyone else wanna give it a shot?"

Louie waited so that one of her peers had a shot at receiving accolades for getting the right answer, but the room remained quiet.

As Mr. Richards looked around, Louie couldn't suppress her urge to speak up any longer. She raised her hand, and the teacher pointed in her direction.

Louie took a deep breath and spoke.

"If you define *deadliest* based on percentage of the population that was killed, then the deadliest war ever fought on American soil was King Philip's War, from 1675 to 1678. The war was named after Massasoit's youngest son, Metacom, who assumed the name King Philip to pay homage to the initial friendly relations between the Native Americans and the Plymouth colonists. Over time, the relationship eroded and war broke out, which cost the colonists approximately thirty percent of their population, while the Indians suffered nearly double that number."

Mr. Richards smiled.

"Excellent, Louie. I'm happy to see that *somebody* read those chapters over the weekend. Okay, onward and upward . . ."

Mr. Richards was interrupted by Principal Sanchez, who walked into the classroom without knocking—a first in his twenty-five years at the school.

"Sorry to interrupt, Mr. Richards. I need Louie Washington to come with me."

The students' eyes widened, and they looked at each other with smirks.

From the back of the room Louie heard "Oooo, someone's in *trouble* . . ."

The class burst out laughing as the hair on the back of Louie's neck stood up straight.

Principal Sanchez turned to Louie. "Please come with me, Miss Washington."

Louie pushed her chair back and gathered her books. She avoided all eye contact with her peers and walked briskly out the door into the humidity of the hallway. Principal Sanchez followed right behind, and when they were out of earshot of the classroom, Louie turned toward him.

"Sir, am I in t-t-trouble?"

She was petrified. The quintessential model student, she had never had to go to the principal's office, with the exception of volunteering periodically to help the school secretary with copying and filing.

The principal's face was grim.

"No, Miss Washington. You're not in trouble."

"Then what's going on?"

She was totally confused.

"Please come with me to the office."

Louie's gut told her to keep quiet and follow instructions.

When they got to the office, Louie could tell that something was seriously wrong. Mrs. Binaca, the school secretary who adored Louie, remained uncharacteristically quiet and did not make eye contact. Principal Sanchez led Louie into his office and purposefully left the door open as he offered her a seat.

"Miss Washington, I don't know how to say this. In my entire career, I've only had to do this one other time, and I prayed it would never happen again. Miss Washington, I'm sorry to tell you that there's been an accident. Your father has passed away."

Louie felt her body melt into the wood of the chair. The clock on the wall stopped ticking.

Principal Sanchez saw Louie staring at him, but he quickly realized she was actually staring *through* him. She grabbed the right arm of the chair and gently poured herself onto the floor as she slowly lost consciousness.

Louie had no idea of how much time had passed when she felt a cold cloth on her forehead. She opened her eyes to see the face of Mrs. Binaca looking at her with sympathetic eyes as she continued to apply the hand towel to Louie's face.

"W-what happened?" asked Louie.

"You fainted, dear. You'll be fine. It's normal. Let me help you back into your chair."

The secretary placed her arm around Louie's left shoulder and helped her back onto the chair. Once she had regained her composure, Mrs. Binaca handed her a bottle of water and left the room.

Principal Sanchez still looked grim.

"Louie, I'm terribly sorry to be the one to tell you this horrible news. I honestly don't know what to say to comfort you. I've known your dad for years, even before you became such a top student here. He was a great man. He loved you kids dearly, and he adored your mom.

"A police officer will be here in about ten minutes to take you home. Your other siblings are being notified as we speak, and someone will be taking them home, as well. I'm going to meet you all there, along with a grief counselor."

Louie felt like she was levitating six inches above the chair. As she floated in her mind, she began to gather her thoughts.

"Mr. Sanchez, what happened? Was it a heart attack? I know his doctor has been concerned about his cholesterol. I've been on him about eating better and knocking off those weekend cigars."

Principal Sanchez leaned against his metal desk.

"Louie, there was an accident."

She looked at the worn hardwood floor and then back at Principal Sanchez.

"I knew it. I knew it, dammit. I *knew* he was gonna get hurt someday out on those damn fishing boats. That damned job! Guys have been dying on Guild Harbor boats forever. Did he fall overboard? Was it a rogue wave?"

Sanchez inhaled slowly and deeply. He didn't want to be the one to tell her this part, but she had a right to know. He didn't trust anyone else to convey the information with the required sensitivity.

"Miss Washington, it wasn't a fishing accident. It had nothing to do with the dangers of his job. It was an overdose. He took too much of some drug. Honestly, I don't know all the details."

"What! Mr. Sanchez, my dad doesn't do *drugs*! It can't be true. He *hates* drugs! He keeps my brothers away from anyone in the neighborhood who might be involved in that trash! As do I. I watch them like a hawk!"

Sanchez sat down in the chair next to Louie.

"Again, I don't know all the details, dear. The police should have more information shortly. They're going to do an autopsy and get to the bottom of exactly what happened. The captain of the boat is positive that his condition was consistent with a drug overdose."

Louie stared at the eggshell ceiling.

Autopsy.

The word stung Louie like a thousand hornets.

CHAPTER THIRTY-TWO

Aboard the *American Wake*

As Justin was trying to fall asleep, he could hear Marlene's deep breathing. He'd been noticing over the past several nights that her sleep patterns had changed. She was resting heavier and her breathing was more pronounced. He knew that the pregnancy was interfering with her normal biorhythms, and her body was responding by making her work harder at the basics.

He rolled over onto his left side and buried his face in the pillow. He'd been thinking a lot about his late uncle, Rick, and tonight was no exception.

As a young boy, Justin had experienced the horror of witnessing his beloved uncle being gunned down during an afternoon stroll. A car had pulled over, asking for directions, when suddenly one of the passengers opened fire and assassinated the man Justin adored. The vision of the hit had haunted his nightmares ever since. On that day Justin decided to go to war with the *world*.

He surrendered to sleep after about five minutes and was soon immersed in a dream.

He was walking through a dank, dark swamp. The mosquitoes feasted on any speck of exposed flesh, and when they bit him, blood streamed down his face and hands. As he walked, the damp moss caressed his cheeks and rendered a strange comfort.

Occasionally he tripped on one of the many thick roots that reached out of the ground like a corpse's arm trying to escape a burial plot. He was on a mission, however, and no roots or insects were going to thwart his efforts.

Two little girls steadfastly followed him about thirty yards to his rear. They reminded him of two similar characters in a Stephen King / Stanley Kubrick film. They would yell out to him, "Daddy. What are you doing? What are you looking for?"

This infuriated him. He was trying to concentrate on his mission.

"Girls! How many times do I have to tell you? I'm not your father! I don't have any children. I had two, but I killed them. I kilt them real good, as they say in the swamplands. Now, leave me alone. G'won. Git!"

"No, Daddy. We don't like it in the clouds. It's not a nice place. We'd rather be here with you and watch you do whatever it is you're doing."

He was unnerved by the way the two spoke in tandem, but he wasn't going to let that deter his focus. He proceeded toward the pond where Uncle Rick was waiting and in need of his help. He had to save Uncle Rick from the crocodiles.

After another quarter of a mile of brushing aside the hanging moss and swatting the mosquitoes with the razor-sharp teeth, Justin reached the shore of the swamp.

The water had a stale odor, and a thin film covered the surface. In the middle of the pond was Uncle Rick, lying on his back, doing the dead man's float.

"Uncle Rick!" he yelled. "Are you okay?"

Rick put his finger to his lips and replied, "I'm okay, boy. Just keep quiet. I'm trying to not disturb these crocs that are all around me. They keep circlin', but they won't bite me as long as I remain still. You should play statue too, Justin. Stop traipsing through this godforsaken piece of Earth. Who are those little girls behind you?"

"I'm not sure, Uncle Rick. They say they're my daughters."

"That's strange, Jus. You don't have any daughters. You killed them. Remember?"

"Yes, Uncle Rick. I remember. I think that's why I'm stuck in this swamp. God is punishing me for that."

"Boy, God punishes us all for doing bad things. It's kinda His thing. We're taught that he loves us, but don't piss him off!" Rick chuckled.

"Uncle Rick, I'm gonna start shooting these crocs and then you can swim to shore, and we can try and find a way outta here."

"Boy, you don't get it. You can shoot these damn crocs all you want, but they just keep coming back. And even if they stop coming back, there still ain't no way outta here. This is it."

From behind, he heard the girls call out to him simultaneously, "See Daddy. See. There's no way out of this swamp. We're here with you. We're here with you for eternity. We're never leaving, and neither are you."

"Stop calling me your daddy! I'm nobody's daddy!"

Rick started swatting some feisty insects which caused him to thrash in the water. The circling crocodiles became agitated and decided it was time to teach this old guy a lesson. Justin readied the rifle that he had slung over his shoulder. He bent down on one knee and peered into the laser scope.

BANG! BANG!

The shots were muffled due to the thickness of the air. He began popping the crocodiles in their heads. He was deadly accurate, and the giant reptiles, once hit in the brain, would roll over in the putrid water so all he could see was the light yellow of their upturned bellies. He continued to shoot and kill.

"Daddy!" the girls clapped their hands, "you're great at killing! Can you teach us how to kill like that? We'd like that, Daddy."

He paused, turned around, and yelled, "Stop calling me Daddy, you two!"

He had turned back to aim the rifle once again when he noticed that the dead crocs had disappeared and the swamp was once again filled with dozens of similar beasts who were very much alive and growing ever more aggressive.

It was then that he noticed two of the crocs heading right for Uncle Rick.

He aimed the weapon at the two rogues but realized his rifle had jammed. In a panic, he began dismantling the hardware in order to find the spot that was stuck, but it was too late.

The crocs descended on Uncle Rick and began tearing him to pieces.

"No!" screamed Justin. "No! Uncle Rick!"

Rick's right leg and left shoulder were in the mouths of the two attackers, who continued to bite and thrash.

He was shocked at how calm Rick was.

"Boy, this is just what happens," his uncle said. "It's no big deal, Justin. This is what happens when you go to Hell. It's all in the brochure, kid," said Rick, as his appendages were slowly being ripped from his torso.

"No! Uncle Rick!"

He heard the little girls behind him. "See, Daddy. Uncle Rick is right. It's just what happens in Hell. We were in our Hell alone, but now we're in Hell with you! See, we're all together in Hell."

"What!" Justin shot up in bed. He felt the sweat drip into his eyes from his wet forehead, and he rubbed the cold perspiration from his forearms.

He looked around the boat's master stateroom. It was just another nightmare.

He looked to his right and Marlene was sleeping. The only sound in the room was her heavy breathing as she inhaled and exhaled in metronomic syncopation.

CHAPTER THIRTY-THREE

Joist's Marine Gear and Tackle Shop, Guild Harbor

As Amina walked into the tackle shop, all she could smell was the warm scent of history.

Joist's family business was fourth-generation Guild Harbor, and nothing short of a mini institution. For a century, fishermen with fouled-up longlines had been showing up at Joist's to get fresh gear that would put them back out on the water.

The shop was now run by one of the great grandsons, nicknamed Pound. Nobody really knew what that meant, but local lore said that's what he'd do to a customer if he didn't pay his bill on time. In Guild Harbor, you settled your tabs if you sought longevity.

Amina walked in tentatively. She was nervous by nature, and that feeling was taken to a new level today because of why she was here and what she'd been told to purchase.

She walked around the aisles pretending to be interested in Pound's wares until the proprietor lost patience with what he perceived to be Amina's snooping.

"Ma'am," said Pound, "I'm happy to help, but I gotta know what you're lookin' for."

"Oh, yes," replied Amina. "My brother just bought a big cabin cruiser, and he sent me to fetch him some bumpers. You know, to protect the boat when it hits the dock?"

Pound chuckled. "You mean *fenders*, ma'am. Fenders. Bumpers are on an amusement park ride. Fenders are on a vessel or a dock. Kinda like a *map* is what's in a car while a *chart* is what you find on a boat."

Amina nodded. "Oh, I see. Okay. I need some big fender nettings.

You know, the sheaths that go around the things. You see, my brother is bringing the plastic. He sent me to buy the socks that wrap around them so they don't scuff the boat."

Pound shrugged. "Sure. Come right this way. Any color preference?"

"Yes, thank you for asking. Black, if you have any in stock?"

"Yeah, I think I have some out back. How many?" asked Pound.

"Three."

"I think I can help you out. Just give me a few minutes. I apologize if this sounds forward, but might it be possible to get your phone number?"

Amina paused. "No disrespect, sir, I'm not sure how long I'm going to be in town."

CHAPTER THIRTY-FOUR

Guild Harbor Men's Club

Seeing Captain Louie Washington walk into the Guild Harbor Men's Club was tantamount to catching a glimpse of Halley's Comet.

She nodded hellos to those she recognized, some of whom she had arrested in the past for "drunk and disorderly." Tonight, she had a different mission. She was in search of Chico Main and the Risottos. Nobody gave Louie any flak. That typically ended badly for the instigator.

She finally found Chico Main holding court in a dark corner. The dealer immediately reacted.

"Captain. Everything okay? Everyone here is peaceful and law-abiding," said Chico as his cronies chuckled. "How can I help you?" Main's voice had dropped an octave.

Louie sat down at the round table next to Chico. The waitress approached and Louie requested a ginger ale.

"Chico, I need your help with that project we talked about."

Chico motioned to his flunkies to beat it.

Louie paused until they'd left, then continued.

"I don't have my arms around the whole thing yet. We know Scola's up to something, as we discussed. If I can prove that it's him behind all the shit that's been going on recently, we'll raid his wannabe museum tonight. What I need is confirmation from you and your guys that it's gonna go down. Are you involved? Speak now, Chico. Speak the truth, because if you don't, your next chance will be yelling from behind steel bars."

Chico sat back and rubbed his three-day-old stubble.

"Easy, easy . . . I dunno, Captain. Jib's ambitious. Word around the wharf is that he has some out-of-town talent involved."

Louie tilted her head while surveying Chico's eyes, then responded.

"Okay, you know that some new drug is coming in. How about helping me in a few hours? Ya know, just point out the incoming vessel with the shipment? Just toss a finger, and then you and your partners are free to go. Nobody will ever know you were there."

Chico was taken aback.

"If I rat out Jib on his run, I'm gonna end up in a crab trap. I ain't afraid of Scola himself, but he's got the money to permanently squelch anyone who talks."

Louie saw her angle.

"I understand. How about this—I'll make sure that any drug charges currently against you and your clowns wash up on the Island of Missing Files? Happens all the time in an understaffed police station, with all the budget cuts. Shit . . . we're lucky we have toilet paper."

Chico ran his ringers through his greasy hair.

"Okay, whadda we gotta do?"

Louie paused. "Meet me down at the Kirkman docks where they're supposed to pull up with the new drug."

"Okay, me and the Risottos. We help you, then we gotta clean slate in this town?"

Louie laughed out loud. "Yeah, your slate will be washed. That will probably last all of two days, but yes, I'll see that you get a fresh start."

Chico nodded in a sign of appreciation.

"You will meet up with one of my undercover officers," said Louie. "Just do what she says, complete the assignment without incident, and I will hold up my end of the bargain."

Chico felt like he'd just hit the Powerball without even having to pay the two bucks.

CHAPTER THIRTY-FIVE

Kirkman Docks, Guild Harbor

Chico spoke first.

"This is cool, guys. Taking a gig to gut-punch that arrogant bastard, Scola. Might make him late on this month's Ferrari payment."

He shared a chuckle with Pete and Paul Risotto, who rarely showed much thought or emotion. Clearly, Chico captained this ship of fools.

Paul interjected, "Chico. Scola ain't gonna be happy when he finds out that it was us who ratted him out. Guy's got money."

Chico waved the words out of the air. "No, you waste of air. Scola ain't gonna find out. We're being protected by Louie. We're friggin' Teflon."

"What's Teflon, chief?" asked Peter.

Chico ignored what he hoped was a rhetorical question.

He was excited. Chico loved action, and it was welcoming for him to be running a dock-side score. He was happy that for once, he was on the *right* side of the law, albeit for selfish reasons. He knew that helping Louie Washington could only benefit someone in Guild Harbor who might need an indiscretion to slide into an outgoing tide.

Chico heard the clip-clop of a woman's shoes coming down the dock.

"Hi guys," the woman said, "Nice night. Thanks so much for helping with this assignment."

"No problem. Thank *you* for the invitation," said Chico to the presumed undercover police officer. "What exactly is it that you want us to do?"

"Just do as Louie asked. When Scola's delivery vessel is in sight, just point her out. Then, screw."

Chico nodded. This was far from heavy lifting. However, in this moment of playing temporary deputy, he couldn't keep his mouth shut.

"Officer, I can save us some time. I didn't tell Louie this at the bar 'cause I wanted to make sure this whole scene was on the level. Through my contacts, I can already tell you the exact description of the vessel. We really don't need to wait around."

The woman was surprised by this information, but she appreciated the efficiency of moving things along.

While the Risottos remained quiet, Chico launched into a full detailed description of *Booty Call*. The woman wrote nothing down but made vivid mental notes.

When Chico was finished, he folded his arms in satisfaction with a job well done.

"How's that, Officer? That detailed enough? It's everything but the damn hull number."

The woman smiled. "You guys did great, Chico. Louie will be pleased."

Somewhere out of the dark from roughly ten yards away, Chico and both Risottos were hit with silenced nine-millimeter pops into their three heads, the slugs plopping into the harbor.

Despite the New England night air, the three heads still took about four minutes to cool.

Amina looked over the carnage. She was in shock despite knowing in advance what was going to transpire. She found herself steeped in guilt, even though she wasn't the one who had pulled the trigger.

At that moment, memories of her dead son pelted her like an annoying rain.

CHAPTER THIRTY-SIX

Dunlap Neck

Scola walked his grounds after building a stiff Ketel & Cran. He gazed across the harbor devoid of any real thoughts. Although the gentle breeze was a bit chilly, all Jib felt was heat.

He had a strange feeling of trepidation, which was unlike his usual cavalier approach to his business. He feared that he had enjoyed it too well, and for too long.

He noticed the grass was getting a little long, as it tended to do with the harbor front moisture. He shook his drink. The jingle of ice cubes was a song.

He walked down toward a wooded area surrounded by rocks that were glacier puzzle pieces.

The trees swayed. The leaves danced with the wind.

But not *all* of the leaves.

Jib dropped his glass as he recognized the form, even in death.

He walked over to see the body of Eel Korvitz hanging by the largest branch.

Pinned to his chest was a note. *Your tab, Skip.*

CHAPTER THIRTY-SEVEN

Beverly Hospital, Beverly, Massachusetts

"Ms. Dunn, the technician is ready to see you now. Please follow me," said the tech assistant as she led Marlene down a long hallway to the ultrasound examination room.

Marlene savored the surreal moment. A year ago, as she knelt on the marina dock at gunpoint in Jekyll Island, Georgia, she never would have dreamt that twelve months later she would not only still be alive, but ready to give life.

While there were other prenatal care options on the North Shore, the doctor that she consulted in Guild Harbor had recommended Beverly Hospital as the best maternity unit in the area. She took his advice, and now here she was, about to see her unborn baby for the first time.

She was disappointed that Justin was not with her, but she forgave his absence, knowing he was immersed in serious business with Shark and Peeler. While she worried about Michonne being exposed to the dangers of Justin's dealings, she was proud of her for having grown into a formidable, independent woman at such a young age. Most mothers would be horrified at the education that Michonne was receiving from her dad, but Marlene was not most mothers. On more than one occasion, Michonne had already witnessed firsthand the horrors that humanity can dole out. She was grateful that she and Justin had been preparing the young girl to face any challenge.

The tech assistant's hand motioned toward a gurney. "Please lie down and make yourself comfortable. The technician will be along in just a few minutes."

"Thank you," replied Marlene as she lay down on the cold, plastic mattress. She'd always hated the feel of gurney paper on her body. The callous feeling, coupled with the crunch of the liner, reminded her that she was sick. Although this time it was not an illness that had brought her to a hospital, but rather a happy occasion.

Marlene had been researching prenatal ultrasounds online prior to her appointment, and the process fascinated her. She found it interesting that the tests used high-frequency sound waves, inaudible to the human ear, transmitted through the abdomen via the transducer to view inside. With prenatal ultrasound, the echoes would be recorded and transformed into video images of Marlene's unborn child.

Marlene also knew that the procedure could pick up any major anatomical abnormalities or birth defects—but she wouldn't let herself hold those thoughts.

The door opened and the technician entered the room.

"Congratulations, Mom," said the technician with a warm smile. "I'm Linda, and I'll be handling today's test. We're gonna have some fun. Jane, can you get some more gel?" The technician smiled at Marlene. "Just make yourself comfortable. This certainly won't hurt, but I'll be pressing hard at times so that that we can get some really great pictures. Sound good?"

"Sounds great. You're the boss," replied Marlene, with a touch of nervousness.

The assistant handed the gel to the technician, who applied it generously to Marlene's belly. Marlene was about fourteen weeks pregnant, so this was an early ultrasound. She was eager to see her unborn child, and the doctor had recommended it, since she was going to be forty soon.

The technician maneuvered the device across Marlene's belly as she stared at her large color monitor. Marlene watched in anticipation as the images of her insides took shape on the screen.

"Ah," said the technician. "There he is!"

Marlene was awestruck.

In a year when she'd seen so much death, now she was seeing new life and new beginnings.

"It's a boy?" asked Marlene.

"Sure is. Everything looks normal. It's still early, but I don't see anything of concern."

Marlene was floating. This was her son! She had nobody to pray to, but for a brief moment, she wished for her baby to lead a peaceful life. A life that did not involve taking up his father's vocation, which was in the process of swallowing her adopted daughter.

CHAPTER THIRTY-EIGHT

Booty Call **Returning to Guild Harbor**

Shark and Peel were fortunate to have enjoyed a light following sea for most of the ride home. After the long journey back from the Canadian rendezvous, Shark spoke up.

"Hey Peel, we're about to round the breakwater and enter the harbor. Make sure you hail Justin."

Peel responded, "Aye, Skip."

"And Peel," Shark yelled. "He's got his daughter with him, so be cool. Keep it subtle."

"No prob, Cap."

Peeler grabbed the ship-to-shore mic, and then thought better of it, deciding he should contact Justin by cell phone. He tapped in the digits.

"Hey, Justin, just checking in. We're roundin' the breakwater now. Meet us at the Kirkman docks?"

After a crackle due to the sketchy connection, Justin responded. "Sounds good, Peel. We have a visual, and I have protection looking over you. Tell Shark to come in slow like a pro."

"That's a roger, Jus."

While things were going smoothly, Peeler was still nervous. Yeah, they had the drugs and a solid payday ahead, but something didn't feel right in his gut.

Peeler remembered back to when he was a kid growing up in Ocala, Florida. It was a quiet place—definitely could be dubbed the middle of nowhere. He thought back to when he was around ten years old and was riding his bike home from the local park, back to his mom's trailer. He had never known his dad, nor had he ever been that curious. His mom was working hard waitressing to provide for them. Peeler had learned early on that even though the other kids always teased him, he possessed the skills of a survivor.

He thought back to this one particular day when he was coming home from a pickup baseball game and it was so hot that it hurt his legs when they brushed up against the side of his bike as he pedaled. The day was calm, soon to be nightfall, when the Florida summer temperature would let up a bit.

He had taken the usual trail through an old orange grove long since abandoned by the owners, who'd had to jettison the business following an early frost the previous autumn. As he pedaled, he smelled the sour scent of old orange trees and heard the squawking of birds. He felt a rare moment of peace for a kid whose nerves were always on edge.

As he rode along, he gauged that he was about ten minutes from his trailer when his senses shifted color. He suddenly didn't feel alone. Through the sound of the squawking birds, he heard the grumbling of motorbikes, which could only mean one thing.

The Walter brothers.

Peeler immediately went into defensive mode. He pedaled faster as he felt the sweat sting his already sun-glared eyes.

"Let's get him!" yelled Tick Walter as the motorbikes quickly caught up with skinny Peeler on his old bicycle.

Peeler pedaled in a frenzy. He was able to take a hard right off the trail that he knew was a beeline back to his trailer.

The Walter brothers kept yelling, "Hey retard boy! We just wanna talk!"

When the first rock thrown by Tick Walter pelted off the back of Peeler's head, he immediately felt a wetness that dripped down the nape of his neck. Adrenaline took control of Peeler's bicycle as he maneuvered through the thick woods that he knew blindfolded.

Peeler shook off the bad memory. His thoughts returned to Guild Harbor.

Shark slowed the boat to no-wake speed as he entered the harbor and made a course for the Kirkman docks.

It was Peeler's job to scan the harbor and report back to Shark if he spotted any visible hazards, as the North Shore's rocky coast was still unfamiliar to the captain.

Shark checked in. "Hey, Peeler. All okay out in front? Nothing sticking out?"

"Nah, Skip. Looks like plenty of water. Let's just get to the dock. I'm exhausted."

Shark kept the course toward the inner harbor so that he would land at the dock unnoticed. As he took the vessel out of gear in order to slow down, he noticed that the fenders tied to the dock were strangely shaped and unusually thick.

"Peel!" yelled Shark. "Are we okay to land here? All clear?"

Peel wasn't sure how to respond, but he knew that calm was king.

"Don't worry, Skip. Let's just make her fast."

Shark spun the vessel to welcome a portside tie-up, and to hopefully get rid of the cargo quickly. He just wanted a payday, and an end to transporting for Jib Scola.

As Shark spun the boat, he noticed the portside stern hit one of the fenders, which emitted an especially rough *crunch* sound. Shark looked to his left at the first fender that he'd hit, and then immediately gazed to midship and bow on the port side.

"Holy shit." Shark was speechless for a moment. "Peel. P-Peel. What the—"

Peeler thought his boss was overreacting to a little smack against the dock, but he took a look over the port side of the vessel out of curiosity.

Three fenders had been placed there to block the boat from hitting the dock too hard. However, these fenders were not made of rubber or vinyl. Instead, each was filled with a human head, from Chico Main and Pete and Paul Risotto.

Instinctive thoughts struck Shark's head like lightning.

"Peel, we're being fuckin' ambushed!"

Peel froze as Shark yelled into the radio, "Justin, Justin, we need backup! I repeat—need help! It's an ambush!"

The first bullet entered Peeler's lower arm and exited into part of the vessel's fiberglass. He yelled in pain, "Skip, I'm hit!"

Shark spun the boat around, but not before the boat's canvas was hit with two more shots, while yet a third skimmed his shoulder.

"Peel!" yelled Shark. "Get down!"

Peeler jumped deep into the cockpit of the vessel to avoid any more fire.

Shark did his best to extricate the vessel from this disaster, but it was all happening too fast.

"Shark! Shark!" Justin screamed into the radio.

"Jus, there's crazy shit going down! I'm not sure what's happening. Peeler is hit, and I got skimmed. We're aborting! Gonna head over to Jib's house and dump the stash. Call him! I just tried to dock the boat against three severed heads!"

On the other end, Justin just shook his head. "All right—but forget Jib's house! It's all rocks. Time for a quick Plan B. It's low tide, so head under the Bunker Bridge and meet me at the marina, where you've been staying. I'll get transportation."

Peel, in a moment of clarity, yelled back at his captain. "Skip, the fix was in for this! Who pulled this shit?! Just get us out of the harbor and back to the marina! We're sitting ducks here! My fuckin' arm hurts like shit! The only time I like gettin' shot is when I'm drunk!"

Shark obliged by banging down on the engines' hammers and heading for the marina.

Meanwhile, Justin called Jib Scola. The call was ignored, but he kept dialing until a tired-sounding Jib Scola picked up.

"Yeah, Jus. What's up? Is everything going smooth?"

Justin boomed, "Yeah, Jib! Real fuckin' smooth! We got people getting shot down here! Get one of your goddamned drivers out of bed. I want a car at Shark's marina in five minutes—not six, you lazy fuck!"

Jib was startled. "Wait, Jus. What's happening?"

"For once, Jib, just shut the fuck up and do as your told, you waste of space! Get the driver to the marina to pick us up!"

Jib didn't respond, merely dropped the call and hit speed dial to connect with one of his most trustworthy 24/7 guys.

The *Booty Call* ignored the speed limit under the bridge and tied up at the marina to assess the situation. Shark was freaking out because he knew the cops would be there any minute and he needed to get rid of the dope. He wasn't going to come this far and not deliver the goods and get paid.

Justin and Michonne followed *Booty Call* and tied up at the dock.

Justin looked at Peeler, and then at Shark.

"You gotta get Peel to the hospital. I don't wanna call an ambulance and attract attention, but he needs help. Fast. Jib is sending transport. We'll have him drive Peel to Adams-Graham and then dump us and the dope at Scola's. Looks like Peel's got one in the arm, and you in the shoulder. You all right?"

"Yeah, we'll live, but Peel's gotta get patched," said Shark.

Peeler was losing blood and growing pale.

"I'm gonna take him around the corner and call 911. Jus, you wait here for the car. Get the damn dope outta here!"

Shark turned to Peeler. "Hey, buddy, just say that you got mugged while going for a late-night smoke. With all the shit that's been going down in this town lately, they'll believe you. C'mon, I'll bring you around the corner."

"Whatever you say, Shark," responded a weakened Peeler.

CHAPTER THIRTY-NINE

Louie Washington's GHPD Cruiser

They sat quietly for several minutes until Louie finally broke the silence. "This was a bad night. People died," said Louie to the head of the operation. "Lotta people dying, and I don't see any end in sight. Just gonna get worse. No need for it," Louie lamented to "the General"—her nickname for the one in charge.

The General continued to look straight ahead. "Louie, don't tell me that you're starting to go soft. People die *every* night. What makes this evening so different? Are you starting to lose focus on our mission?"

Louie looked at the General. "Screw you for saying that! Going soft . . . Shit. I'm the one doing all the damned dirty work. I'd like to see you out on the front lines for some of this shit."

It was not like Louie to lose her cool, but the level of violence over the past week had frazzled her well-hardened heart.

"I want you to read something," said the General. "It's a report from the National Institute on Drug Abuse. Go ahead. Read it. See what our mission is about."

Louie took the piece of paper and pulled out a penlight.

Every day, more than 130 people in the United States die after overdosing on opioids. The misuse of and addiction to opioids—including prescription pain relievers, heroin, and synthetic opioids, such as fentanyl—is a serious national crisis that affects public health as well as social and economic welfare. The Centers for Disease Control and Prevention estimates that the total "economic burden" of prescription opioid misuse alone in the United States is $78.5 billion a year, including the costs of healthcare, lost *productivity, addiction treatment, and criminal justice involvement.*

How did this happen?

In the late 1990s, pharmaceutical companies reassured the medical community that patients would not become addicted to prescription opioid pain relievers, and healthcare providers began to prescribe them at greater rates. This subsequently led to widespread diversion and misuse of these medications before it became clear that these medications could indeed be highly addictive. Opioid overdose rates began to increase. In 2017, more than 47,000 Americans died as a result of an opioid overdose, including prescription opioids, heroin, and illicitly manufactured fentanyl, a powerful synthetic opioid. That same year, an estimated 1.7 million people in the United States suffered from substance use disorders related to prescription opioid pain relievers, and 652,000 suffered from a heroin use disorder (not mutually exclusive).

Louie was quiet.

The General grunted and said, "Like I told you—I fear that you're going soft on me. Listen, Louie, someone in my position can't be running around the docks at midnight. It would blow my cover and thus scuttle all of our efforts. It could queer everything that we've worked for. The fact that I am who I am is what makes us a success."

Louie shifted her body to face the General, who sat on the passenger side, smoking a cigar. "Can you open the window? That thing stinks."

The General also shifted to better face Louie.

"Dear, must you complain so much? The stress of this mission is really starting to chip away at your sense of decorum. Please, we're professionals."

The General pressed a button and the window opened to greet the night air.

"Happy?" asked the General.

"Ecstatic," replied Louie, who wiped her mouth as if in frustration.

"Ya know, I wonder what my dad would think of all this," said Louie. "I wonder if he'd be okay with everything I've gotten myself into? I mean, I'm doing it all for him. I'm avenging the death of my father, which is one of the oldest reasons in the world for getting involved in shit like this. It's all for my dad, who loved me."

The General gave a slight head shake and leaned over to gently kiss Louie's lips, who in turn responded with a flicker on her moist tongue. The two caressed each other's necks.

Little did Louie know that the General would kiss a week-old corpse if there were two bits to be made in the deal. Louie had sincerely fallen in love, and naively thought the sentiment was reciprocal.

The General's right hand found Louie's thigh and gently moved to her warmth.

Louie inhaled intensely and the General could feel an invitation.

Louie turned away and leaned back.

"We can't do this right now! This is ridiculous. We're in a police cruiser, for chrissake. We can do anything you want once this is over and we get outta here. I thought that you were gonna take me to Palm Beach? You promised we could stay at The Breakers and drink mojitos and fancy pinot noir. What happened to that plan?"

The General sat back and chuckled. "It's all in the works, my dear. It's all in the works. You just better pack some nasty outfits and bring along your favorite toys."

The two exchanged a deep French kiss. When they stopped, Louie spoke up.

"When can we get our hands on the stuff?"

"Soon, Louie. Soon, my love."

The General kissed Louie's cheek, opened the cruiser door, and disappeared into the misty evening.

CHAPTER FORTY

Dunlap Neck

With Peeler finally off in an ambulance, claiming that he'd been mugged, Justin, Michonne, and Shark jumped in the back of a small box truck along with Jib's contraband.

Justin was impressed by how fast Jib could provide late-night livery. He looked at his adopted daughter.

"Honey, your mom would not be too happy with me right now. Hopefully she's sleeping and dreaming nice dreams. Are you okay?"

"I'm fine, Dad," said Michonne. "It all happened so fast that neither of us had to fire a shot." She paused for a moment. "I hope you're not mad at me. I took one of your Glocks from the boat—I just like having it with me."

Justin couldn't believe what he had done to the young girl's life. However, he did feel better knowing she was armed, just in case further chaos ensued. The reality was that mentally, physically, and emotionally, she was in better shape than he was.

"All right, honey. Keep the safety on and don't let anyone know you have it."

Despite the rumbling and clanking of the car, Shark couldn't help but overhear.

"That's one special little lady you have there, Captain Jus," chuckled Shark.

"Thanks," said Justin. "I just can't wait until the day I'm escorting her to a father-daughter dance instead of to a drug runner's mansion." He looked at Michonne, who just shrugged.

The car lumbered into Jib's circular driveway.

The driver threw the gear into park, and finally broke his silence.

"Okay, folks, last stop. Ride's over. Don't forget your personal belongings, and take small children by the hand."

The driver chuckled, having no idea how close Michonne was to shooting him in the temple at that very moment.

Justin and Michonne got out of the car first while Shark grabbed the drug cache.

"I want to give it to him, Justin. I might just make him choke on it."

"Whatever you say, Shark. Let's just get this over with."

As the group walked up to the wide doorway, Amina watched closely from a grove of trees that hid her from the moonlight. Not knowing what was about to happen terrified her, but at least she didn't have to wait alone.

CHAPTER FORTY-ONE

Mary Ann Scola, Boston College Mailroom

Walking down the hall to the mailroom was always depressing for Mary Ann Scola. Damn corridors were snaked, and the lights were half screwed in.

Would be easier to see a toad in the weeds.

"Hi, Shaun," said Mary Ann as she walked down the hall. "How goes it in your world?"

Shaun Greene turned to greet her, checking his shirt buttons. The awkward biology major yearned for the day he'd be able to muster the courage to ask for a date with the prettiest girl on campus.

"Great, Mary Ann. I'm just off by one button today," he said with a smile.

"I dunno, Shaun. I think you look great. Got any good mail?"

"Probably just bills, as always."

The two smiled at each other and went about their business.

Mary Ann tossed her back pack on the floor in order to retrieve the code to her box. She pulled out an old-school yellow Post-it with the code written on it and popped the door.

She found some solicitations from various credit card companies, as well as ads for pizza delivery and the like.

"Hey, Mary Ann!" cried her neighbor, four mailboxes to her starboard side. "What's in there? You must be popular!"

Mary Ann chuckled. "Just some junk mail. Who knows? Maybe I won the lottery."

As she shuffled through her mail she noticed a large envelope that was marked overnight delivery. The return address was her dad's on the North Shore.

She ripped open the package.

Inside was a simple, plastic frame that contained song lyrics from Pink Floyd, plus a note:

[begin ext]

Mary Ann,

My darling. My little girl.

Please accept this gift. I'm not sure how else I can send my love. I've never been good at that. But, as your dad, I want you to know that I love you.

By the way, poems and beautiful lyrics often bring forth tremendous gifts. But you gotta explore the words . . .

Dad

Mary Ann read the note three times, then the lyrics to "Eclipse" from Pink Floyd's *Dark Side of the Moon.*

Then she threw everything to the floor and ran from the mailroom.

CHAPTER FORTY-TWO

Jib Scola's Study, Dunlap Neck

Jib Scola met his smugglers at the door and waved them in without saying a word.

The group meandered through the mansion and ended up in Jib's study, which was where the drug runner felt the safest.

Jib spoke the first words.

"Thanks for comin'. You all look like shit." Jib's eyes were immediately trained on the parcel that Justin held.

Shark was just about to relieve their host of his forehead but realized it might be bad for business.

It was Justin who threw the package across the floor to Jib's feet.

"There you go," said Justin. "Your heroin, your fentanyl, your new *Tsulio*, or whatever else is in this package. Go nuts with it. We did our part, and we're more than finished."

The room remained silent until Shark spoke up, clearly furious.

"Jib, what the hell? We were making a leisurely run and we start catching lead? I got one sore shoulder, and a first mate who's in the ER. I thought you were a big shot in this town and had things bundled. What's with the friggin' rumpus, Skip?"

Jib was quiet and looked out toward the harbor before meeting Shark's eyes.

"I don't know. That's all I have for you. I don't friggin' know. I don't expect you to trust my words, but the truth is that it was not supposed to go down like this. Understand—this is still a small town, with a rumor mill that loves grist. Word gets out."

Michonne was quiet but finally spoke up.

"Dad, I think I'm gonna be sick. Captain Jib, can I use your bathroom?"

"Of course, dear," responded Jib, "it's right off the kitchen to your left."

"Thanks," said Michonne, who held her stomach as she walked toward the kitchen entrance.

Justin, with his assassin's attention to detail, was suddenly curious.

"Hey, Jib. Speaking of the kitchen, where's that maid of yours?"

"I dunno," said Jib. "She comes and goes as she pleases."

Justin's gut was telling him that there was a strange correlation between Amina's absence and all of the crazy events that had been occurring.

"There's something strange about that woman, and you don't seem to see it," said Justin. "Lemme ask you a question. When she's busy in the kitchen, is there any way she can eavesdrop while you're here on the phone?"

Jib pursed his lips. "McGee, if you are insinuating that Amina had anything to do with tonight's fiasco, you're crazy. I'm afraid you've seen too many conspiracy shows on Netflix."

"Maybe," replied Justin, "but I find it odd that she disappears at all hours and you have no idea where she goes. Doesn't take a park ranger to sniff a trail."

As Justin's voice trailed off, they could hear the mansion's main door opening and closing, followed by footsteps coming down the long hallway toward the study.

Justin looked at Jib.

"Amina!" shouted Scola. "Where have you been?"

Amina ducked her head into the study and replied, "I was just visiting a friend, Captain. I'm sorry if you needed something. I'm actually tired and would just like to go to bed."

Jib looked at Shark and Justin.

"Okay, Amina. Have a good night."

The air in the room immediately changed.

"Hey, lady, hold on a minute," said Justin. "Sit down! Throw your handbag in the middle of the floor and put your hands on your knees—and don't move, or I'll blow them off." Justin had pulled out a Smith and Wesson Classic 29. "It would be pretty difficult to prepare Jib's omelets in the morning with only elbows."

While Scola's eyes exploded in fury, surprisingly, Amina's did not. She immediately obliged, sitting down politely in an oversized leather chair.

Jib looked at Justin. "What's the meaning of—"

"Be quiet, Jib. Ever tried it? While we're at it, you sit down, too. No, not behind your desk where I can't see your hands. Put your ass over there," said Justin, motioning to a simple wooden chair next to Amina.

The group was quiet for several seconds.

Shark broke the silence. "Your maid is knee-deep in some kinda shit, Jib. Now, I know that Justin is thinking the same. She disappears at night and all of a sudden there are drug dealers dying and bullets peppering my vessel and almost killing me and Peel? We're getting to the bottom of this shit here and now."

Suddenly, the doorbell rang.

Jib's eyes lit up. "Folks, everyone just relax. Let me see who the hell is at my door at this hour."

Shark spoke up. "I'll go with you, Jib. I'm curious as well. I wouldn't be surprised if it wasn't Annie Wilkes at this point."

Shark pulled out a Glock and led Jib out of the study and down the long hall toward the vast foyer. Before opening the door, Jib stepped into a side parlor and looked out the window.

"Shark, there's a police cruiser in my driveway. Shit!"

Shark shot back in a whisper, "Hey, asshole, you have a bale full of drugs two rooms away."

Shark yelled to his partner, "Justin! I'm bringing him back to the study. Cops outside. Keep your gun on him. Let him hide the duffel!"

Shark grabbed Jib's shoulder and quickly marched him back to the study, where Justin took over the monitoring of Jib's movements. Shark returned to the foyer.

The smuggler walked to the door, ran his hands through his hair, and opened the door.

There stood police captain Mary-Louise Washington.

Shark was startled but kept his cool. "May I help you, Officer?"

"It's *Captain* to you, and yes, I'd like to come in," said Louie.

Shark knew by the look in Louie's eyes that it was not the time to start bickering about warrants. Without flinching, and hoping Louie wouldn't notice the blood on Shark's shoulder due to the dark foyer, Shark said, "Of course, Captain. Please come in."

"Enough of the pleasantries. Where's Scola?" said Louie.

"We're all relaxing in the study. Right this way," said Shark.

"Whaddya doin', taking tea? And what do you mean by *we*?"

"Just a few friends of Jib's. Come on in. I'm sure he'll be happy to see you."

Shark didn't know what to say or do. The whole scene was uncharted territory. He missed the days back in Florida when it was easy to tell the good guys from the bad. He knew that to get arrested was not an option, but he didn't feel like murdering a cop at this particular moment.

Shark and Louie walked down the hall in silence and entered the study.

Justin hid his gun in the back of his belt. Jib and Amina remained still. They knew that Justin could open fire at a moment's notice.

When Scola saw Louie, his eyes ballooned.

"Captain Washington. This is a pleasant surprise. What brings you out at this time of night?"

Louie surveyed the room and noticed Justin's serpent eyes.

"Well, Jib, there has been some chatter about your involvement in certain activities tonight. You've been fortunate for a long time in that we've left you alone. That time is over. Word has it that you're inviting a new kid into town. From what I hear, it's some potent shit."

Jib remained calm. "Well, what is it you want? Look around. We're not doing anything illegal, and I don't see that you're waving a warrant. I think I wanna call my lawyer."

Louie continued to survey the room. "No, Scola. For this assignment, a warrant is not necessary. Where's the dope? Better yet, fuck your usual pansy powder. Where's the *new* dope?"

Jib looked indignant.

"Captain Washington, I have no idea what you're getting at."

Louie removed her badge and threw it on an end table. She then drew a pistol that was clearly not her service revolver. To Justin, it looked like a handgun designed to take down a rhino.

Louie smiled.

"With that toss of a piece of metal, Scola, consider me *off-duty.* Oh, the arrogance. Did you think that I'd watch you run your operation these past few years and quietly sit by like I was watching a polo match at Myopia?"

Jib just stared back. "I don't know what you mean, Captain Washington."

"Enough of the *Captain Washington.* You know I go by Louie, and with my badge off, you can see that I'm now officially a civilian. You can also see that I'm armed and will have no problem with blowing your head clean off."

Jib looked at his maid. She sat still and appeared way too calm.

"Amina, what the hell is going on? Are Jus and Shark right? Did you have something to do with all of this? What are you doin' to me?"

As Louie surveyed the room, Amina did not look meek or mousy. She had the cold, lifeless eyes of a Great White stalking a seal. A doll's eyes.

"Captain," Amina said, staring at Jib, "your drugs killed my son. I snagged this job with the hope that I would see you pay for your sins and for what you did to my family. The time of reckoning is now."

Justin felt the need to interject and calm the air.

"Okay, folks. I see what's going on here. Louie, was it you who took the shots at us tonight?"

"I don't know who you are or where you're from," said Louie, "but I decide who 'fesses up to what, and when. Sit down and put your hands under your ass. You too, Jib."

The guys did as they were told. Louie had the pointed gun and was looking crazed.

"You see, Jib," said Louie, "my daddy was a Gloucester fisherman. Yeah, we were from Lynn, but my dad spent his life on commercial fishing boats out of Guild Harbor. He was part of this town's backbone! Only he was introduced to smack by one of his fishing buddies, and that was the end of him. I was left with no parents and with brothers to tend to. I've worked my ass off to get where I am. I won't tolerate drugs in this town, and I will *not* tolerate your introducing this new Tsulio to our community. This has nothing to do with being a cop. It has everything to do with being a still-grieving daughter."

Jib was speechless as Louie continued.

"Guys like you suck the life out of a town. For that you need to pay. Turn around."

Jib was still. Shark and Justin just watched in silence. They were armed, but Louie had the easier access to a quick blast, so she was calling the shots.

"Turn around, Jib," repeated Louie. "I want to shoot you in the back just like you do to the addicts that buy your shit. Give me your *back*, Jib. Give me your *spine*, Scola!"

Jib suddenly realized that Louie was unhinged—that she would lay everything on the line to serve punishment.

"Okay, okay," said Jib, "I'm turning around. But wait a minute, Louie—just wait a minute. Now I get it. It was you who killed all those drug dealers! Are you out of your mind?"

"No," said Louie. "Just here to *serve and protect.*"

Louie watched as Jib did an about-face, and at the same time she aimed the gun at Justin and Shark, neither of whom flinched.

"You two," barked Louie, "don't move. I know that you're both packing. Take 'em out. Toss them on the floor next to Amina's bag. Now!"

Justin and Shark exchanged looks, and after a brief moment, obliged.

Amina gulped. She had never wanted things to escalate to this level.

Justin and Shark's relinquishing of their weapons appeared to calm Louie, who now aimed her gun at Jib. "Okay, local boy who made it big, how do you want it?"

Scola was starting to feel faint.

"Louie, it doesn't have to be like this. Take the drugs. Take anything you want. I prob'ly have half a million bucks in the basement safe. Take it all! We can be reasonable here."

Louie acted like she'd heard nothing that Jib had said, and just robotically repeated, "How do you want it, Jib?"

Justin and Shark were statue-still while Jib assumed an alabaster hue. He tried once again to defuse Louie. "Please, just take what you want and I'll leave town within the hour, never to return. Ever. I promise that you'll never see me again."

Louie smirked. She was starting to visibly perspire.

"Yes, Jib. You might end up doing just that."

BANG! BANG!

Louie fired two rounds into Jib's right quadricep.

Scola took the two hits in a daze. He stood up on his left leg, staggered three steps, and crashed into the bay window which looked over the harbor. The glass was bulletproof and didn't shatter. Jib lay on the floor with blood streaming from his right leg. He was in shock and unable to talk.

Shark and Justin remained still.

Louie barked, "Amina! You have the blankets?!"

"Yes, Louie, they're right here in the closet."

Shark and Justin looked on in shock and awe as Amina dragged thick wool blankets out of a nearby closet and proceeded to wrap them around the now-howling Scola. She made sure the blankets were tightly wrapped and covered every inch of his body and head.

With a muffle, the group heard Scola scream, "Louie! What are you doing?"

She chuckled.

"Scola, you ever study psychology?"

CHAPTER FORTY-THREE

Jib Scola's Study

Amina had pulled out some duct tape and began wrapping the blankets tightly around Jib's head and chest, making Jib's muffled screams barely audible.

Shark and Justin remained motionless. With their weapons out of reach, they both realized they were going to be forced to be spectators at this bizarre court of retribution.

"You see, folks, this is a certain discredited procedure called rebirthing therapy," said Louie. "It's a healing process that helps *troubled* individuals."

Shark wasn't sure what was transpiring, but realized he was about to witness Jib's one-way ticket to Hell.

"At the time, this cutting-edge technique was supposed to cure young people of any mental deficiencies. It ended up being a disaster, but that was a long time ago. Therapy practices evolve, and my hope is that tonight, Jib will finally be healed of his mental ailments."

Jib continued to bleed profusely as he writhed on the floor next to the window. He kicked and spun around for about two minutes, attempting to extricate himself from this sick form of therapy that was really just a twisted type of torture. Jib tried to scream through the thick wool, but it was futile. Suddenly the pile of blankets went still.

"See, folks," said Louie, "your fearless leader is now healed and reborn."

Shark and Justin stared at Jib's lifeless body lying pathetically on his mansion floor.

"Okay," said Louie, "who's next? You see, Amina? This is how we clean up Guild Harbor. You gotta do it *old school.* Warrants and court dates don't do the trick anymore. You think I wanted to bring Jib to trial just so he could have the shit tossed out on a technicality? No, Amina. This is how we settle and *sterilize.* This is how we clean a town's soul."

Shark said, "Louie, there is no dope. We have nothing. And you're fucked. You're gonna have to kill everyone in this house and not leave a trace in order to get away with this, and that's gonna be impossible. Jib's cameras filmed your cruiser when you arrived, and that tape is fed to some outside security guys. You're done, Louie."

"If that's the case, then you're making my night much easier," said Louie. "I'll go ahead and kill you all and just save a slug for my own temple. What do I care?"

Louie began to pace.

"But, that's not gonna happen. Is it, Amina? Did you do your job like I instructed?"

"Yes, Louie. All surveillance around the property was dismantled this morning. There is no footage of tonight."

Louie nodded her appreciation.

"*O Captain,* my captains. Who's next?" said Louie. "Maybe you, handsome man?" she said, pointing her pistol at Justin. Louie walked over toward McGee and kept the gun trained on his chest.

"You want to bring drugs into my town. Drugs that killed my daddy. Drugs that killed Amina's boy?"

Amina's fierce glare confirmed that she shared Louie's desire for revenge.

Louie smiled, "Well, we'll find the drugs. But at the moment, it's time for retribution. You first, cowboy," said Louie, "and then your friend." She wiggled the gun in her hand and cocked the hammer.

Suddenly a shot rang out, followed by a vacuum-like *whoosh* that came from Louie's left lung.

Michonne stood in the archway to the kitchen, the Glock cooling in her small hand.

Louie fell to the floor as Shark pounced. He put Louie's left arm behind her head and grabbed a cloth from the end table.

"Hey, Officer, if you behave, I'll stop the bleeding and save your life. If you resist, I'm just gonna let you bleed out and ruin this nice oak floor."

Louie was gasping for air. With each breath, the sound went higher up the tonal scale.

Michonne didn't sense a threat from Amina and placed her weapon at her side. The young girl's instincts were acute. She knew this accomplice was nothing without her master.

Amina fell to the floor and wept. "You're all murderers! Even your children!"

Justin yelled, "Michonne, go into the front hallway and stay out of sight. Watch for anyone coming up the driveway."

"But Dad—"

"Do it!"

Justin turned his attention to Amina. "Hey, you got a car?!"

The maid sobbed and nodded.

"Get Louie to the hospital. Tell them she received a call about suspicious activity in this neighborhood and came out to investigate."

Justin looked at Jib's lifeless body and inhaled deeply.

"Amina!" Justin yelled.

She looked back as a squirrel does to a set of tires.

Justin drew on his experience and draped an umbrella of calm over the situation.

"Amina," said Justin, "do as I instruct with Louie. Nobody will get in trouble. If you deviate in *any* way from my instructions, your death will make Scola's look downright merciful. Are we clear? Hey, *dimwit!* Are we fucking clear?!"

Amina merely stared.

"Bitch! Don't play innocent with me. Please know that I will slice your throat and dip the blade into a glass of merlot prior to taking a sip if you cross me. You'll be found covered in cinder blocks fifty feet under the bay. Just try me."

Even Shark was shocked by how Justin's primal instincts took over as he gained control of the scene.

Finally Amina seemed to regain her awareness of the situation. She looked at Justin with eyes that begged for mercy. "Yes, sir. I'll do just as you say. Captain Washington was on a burglar call that went bad."

Justin calmed down.

"I'm sorry about what happened to your son, Amina. Don't make things worse for yourself. Retribution can only be served in Hell, not in Guild Harbor."

Amina knew this was her chance to get out of the situation alive. Despite her serious wound and the fact that she was having trouble breathing, Louie was still alive and could get to the front door with Amina's assistance.

The maid tried to comfort Louie as she threw the officer's arm over her shoulder and made fast for the front door. "C'mon, Louie—we tried. We really tried."

Once they'd left the mansion, Justin began to assess their status.

"Michonne!" he yelled to his daughter in the hallway. "Get back here!"-

Five seconds later Michonne appeared and sat down in an oversized chair. The gun was out of sight, but within a second's reach.

Justin looked around the room. "Shark, you all right?"

Shark just shook his head. "Yeah, man. Damn! I've been through some crazy shit, but I've never seen someone smothered to death in a blanket."

"Listen, Shark, we gotta get outta here," said Justin. "All of us, and fast. The cops are gonna find a severely wounded police captain at the hospital, and once they get here, they'll be dragging out a dead local legend. Death by suffocation, no less. Shit. We don't need the heat or the drama. Let's roll."

"What about Peeler? He's still in the hospital. What if they connect him to this?"

"Louie won't dare. Amina may have scuttled the video surveillance of the property, but I have all the audio recorded on my phone. Louie's gonna recuperate and take her disability—tax-free, I might add—like a champ. She'll keep her mouth shut," said Justin. "Get your vessel up to Maine and hire some local to come down and fetch Peeler once he feels up to it. Give it at least four days."

Shark looked at Justin. "Hey, what about all that dope? I wanna see what we got. I want my money's worth on this job. Any way we can salvage some payout for all this shit?"

Justin had to think.

"It's under Jib's desk, where he kicked the bag. That's the great thing about a heroin run—you can stash so much of it in such a small place. The Coast Guard will never find it."

Shark nodded. "Fine. Let's see what we got. I want to see how much Tsulio was included. We gotta figure out how to get paid in light of everything that happened tonight."

Justin reached for the bale and threw it onto the table in the middle of the room.

"I know this has been a fiasco, but one run of Tsulio should allow us all to chill out financially for quite a while."

Shark inhaled. "Okay, Jus. Cut her open."

The partners exchanged glances as Justin pulled out a jackknife and took a slice of the duct-taped bale. White powder immediately exploded over the metal blade.

"Wow. That's a lotta shit. The only thing is, how do we know what's Tsulio and what's just the usual heroin?"

Shark shook his head. "I dunno, man. Give it a taste test. See if it tastes any different from the usual shit."

"All right," said Justin. This was going to be the answer to all of his dreams. Slowing down, taking it all in. A score that would secure a future for each of them, for the rest of their days, including Michonne, and the new baby on the way.

Justin looked down at the parcel and marveled. It was a new era. While he wanted to get out, Tsulio was the future, and now he owned the local cops. Maybe he wouldn't leave town *just* yet. There was no way Louie Washington would be able to stop another operation. He could do the right thing and offer monthly payoffs, but with Tsulio, it could all be worth it.

Justin licked his finger and dabbed it into the slice.

He tasted.

Shark watched as Justin's eyes took on a curious expression.

Justin took another taste and sat back in thought.

"Hey, partner. Do you think the Canadians knew this was going to be *the* last run that Scola was ever going to make?"

Shark rubbed the area around his wound, as it was starting to throb.

"Yeah, I think they knew. The plan was to execute this mission and then everybody would go their separate ways. Why?"

"Hmm . . ." Justin muttered to himself.

Shark was confused.

"If you knew that an operation was ending—no doubt, no second thoughts—would you go out with or without a risk hanging over your head for years to come? Ya know what I'm sayin'? Would you want a raven constantly hovering over your shoulder?"

Shark's jaw dropped.

Damn Canucks.

CHAPTER FORTY-FOUR

Aboard the *American Wake*

"How are you feeling, honey?" Justin asked the soon-to-be mother of his child.

"I'm okay. Just a lot of nausea."

"Well, get some rest. We don't need to take off anywhere, anytime soon," assured Justin.

"Where's Michonne?" asked Marlene.

"She's resting in her stateroom. Been a long coupla days."

"Is she okay?" asked Marlene, as she started to sit up. "Was there any danger?"

Justin smiled. "Nah. Cookie-cutter mission. Everyone is fine. Shark hurt his shoulder, but no big deal."

"What about Peeler? Is he okay?"

"Ol' Peel is fine. He resting in the ER."

Marl exploded. "The *what?!* I thought you said it was a smooth outing?"

Justin responded, "Smooth as lava rock."

Marlene chewed on that for a moment and then had to ask—"Jus, did that Jib guy ever get his hands on that new drug he was gunning for? *Tsulio*, I think you said it was called?"

"Funny you should ask, hon," said Justin. "Jib hadn't really taken possession of that bale for too long before all hell broke loose."

He started to chuckle.

"What could you possibly be laughing at?" asked Marlene, simultaneously confused and perturbed.

"Oh, nothing. Listen, hon, Shark and I have to take off for a few days, just tying up a few loose ends from the op. No heavy lifting, nothing crazy. You guys will be fine. If you need anything, just call the Guild Harbor PD and ask for Captain Washington. I'm sure you'll be treated like the queen at the ball."

Marlene was wary. "I don't like the sound of this, but Michonne and I are not exactly helpless. Do what you have to do—just stay outta harm's way."

"Oh, you know me, honey. I'm careful to a fault."

Marlene looked skeptical. "Tell me one thing, Jus—was it all worth it?"

"Yeah, Marl," Justin said, laughing again. "I guess you could say it was all worth it. . . . If you were a pastry chef, that is."

Marlene looked at Justin as if he was coming undone.

"Whaddya mean?"

Justin smiled. "Well, when all is said and done, we did that whole operation for a dozen kilos of Canada's finest confectioners' sugar."

Marlene's jaw dropped.

CHAPTER FORTY-FIVE

Antigonish Harbour, Nova Scotia

"Whaddya think of those Yanks celebrating Canada Day on July first? Damn charlatans," shouted Bryce across the deck to Captain Finn.

Finn chuckled as Dogfish worked on repairing the vessel's generator.

"Fuck 'em. Buncha wannabes."

All was calm in the Canadian Maritimes since the meeting with the Guild Harbor gang. They had been paid well to scuttle the mission, although they realized that their Cape Ann distribution network was most likely defunct. In their mind, the Scola connection had died with Jib's sudden desire to retire and trading the Yank's duffel of cash for a drum of sugar seemed like a fair trade at that point.

They looked at Jib Scola's operation as a high-profile, high-risk type of run. It would be easily replaced by Finn's connections in Vermont. The seasoned captain had had enough of the high seas and figured it would be a lot easier to dump future stashes in the Green Mountain State, which didn't have any real drug laws anyway.

"I dunno, Finn," said a concerned Bryce. "Those Yanks seemed like the real deal. My guess is that they were a little pissed off when they cut open our load of sugar."

"Scola's operation is dead," said Finn. "Now he's gotta deal with that crazy lady cop who paid us off. He's running on fumes and the gas pump is closing. We did all right, gentlemen."

"Yeah, but Finn, it wasn't *really* that cop chick who funded our mission."

Dogfish looked up. "Hey, what are you guys talkin' about? Can someone fill me in here—who *were* we working for?"

As the three Canucks diddled around with their business on board, they failed to notice the sound of footsteps approaching.

Suddenly, Justin and Shark hopped aboard the boat. They landed, stepped back, and released the safeties on their AK-47s.

The three Canadians froze.

Finn looked up and knew that within seconds he could be sliced like provolone.

Shark aimed his weapon at Bryce and Dogfish, while Justin kept his trained on MacLeod.

"Guys," said Justin, "we seem to have a little problem. You see, we just drove a *lotta* miles to hear what you have to say for yourselves. Face it. You fucked us in the ear. And as a reader, I *love* a great story! So, begin."

Bryce stared at Captain MacLeod as if waiting for him to wave a magic wand and get them out of this.

Justin stared at Finn.

"What—nothing to say? I guess it's time for us to bend *you* over the gunnel. So, who's first?" he said with a smile, as Shark trained his weapon on Bryce's forehead.

"W-wait a minute, gentlemen," said Finn. "This can *all* be explained—"

"Oh, I expect to hear it, in great detail," said Justin. "No, I take that back. Not just in detail. I wanna be *entertained*. Actually, don't start just yet. We really need to savor this moment."

Shark gripped his AK and tapped a quick five rounds, blowing off Bryce's left ear.

"*Ahhh!* What the fuck? Oh *God!*" yelled Bryce as he fell to the deck, blood streaming from the left side of his head. His ear wound up stuck in the stern scupper, most likely to remain there until the next strong rain.

Finn's eyes bulged from his head.

"What do you want from us, McGee? Yeah, we snookered you, but it was fair game. We didn't threaten or hurt you, and now you come here and blow my partner's fuckin' *ear* off!"

Justin remained calm.

"No, Finn. That would have been a long drive for just an ear . . ."

The assassin turned, swung his weapon, and fired one second's worth of automatic fire into Finn's knee.

"*Nooooo! Fuck!* What are you doing?!"

"Crippling you, Finn," said Justin. "You will never walk the docks again. You will never turn your face into the wind and think you have the upper hand. Your swagger is now a *stagger.*"

Finn hyperventilated while trying to scream.

"You're fucked," said Justin. "You deserve every miserable second of your last days. You will hobble, and you will never forget me. Every time you stumble or crash into a wall, you will hear my name."

Finn writhed on the deck like a gutted bluefish. "What do you want from us?" he pleaded through his tears and agony.

The darkest part of Justin's soul took command. He was just assuming a delivery role at this point.

"Finn, you bore me. I thought all you folks up here were all witty and shit. You're downright dull conversationalists."

Ratta! Justin plunged another second's worth of automatic fire into Finn's other knee.

Finn could not utter a sound. Shock slid him down onto one side.

Justin looked at him for a solid three seconds.

"Enjoy watching the sea where you will never travel again. You'll live a long life, but it's gonna kinda suck. *King of all he surveys!* Not so much anymore. Maybe they'll get you some kinda forklift and let you board your vessel once in a while."

Justin walked around the deck, reviewing the wounds of his quarry.

"To tell you the truth, Finn, you'll be lucky to not end up on an anchor line within the hour. I'm still trying to decide what to do with you. Maybe just leaving you maimed will suffice?"

Bryce looked at Finn in horror; he didn't dare touch him; he was in such pain.

"Bottom line, guys," said Justin, "who hired you? Who put you up to the stupid, foolish task of screwing us? Did you really think we would just take it in the ass and then go home and sit in a hot bath? Are you nuts, arrogant, or both?"

"Whaddya lookin' at, you fuckin' idiot?" Shark suddenly yelled at Dogfish, who happened to be staring at him the wrong way.

"N-nothing. I'm j-just scared and I don't want to be shot."

"That's unfortunate. Bad day for you. However, a day for reflection. You religious?"

"W-w-what?" stammered Dogfish.

Shark fingered his weapon and pointed it at the mate's ankle. He unleashed the automatic fire and the deckhand's foot ended up on the other side of the deck. It took eight slugs to sever Dogfish's tough tendons.

"*Shit!* What the *fuck!*" screamed Dogfish, in excruciating pain.

The three Canadians all sat there looking pathetic as they nursed their wounds. Maybe one day they would heal, but the reality was, they would never be the same.

"All right, gentlemen," said Justin. "For my next trick, I might start singing 'O Canada'—although I think that might be disrespectful to your fellow honest countrymen who know how to engage in proper international trade. Didn't you pricks sign on to that whole NAFTA deal?"

The three were entering various stages of shock, but Justin was in no mood to be quiet. He was a man of many moods, and right now, the howling was starting to annoy him.

"Now that we've made our point, it's important you know what we want. Fuck it, what we *demand!* As I said, we want to know who put you up to that needlessly dishonest transaction. Was it worth it, Bryce? Perhaps you can't hear me too well?"

Bryce stared up at Justin, begging for mercy. He spoke, but the words were incoherent.

Justin shook his head. "Bryce, my friend, your left ear is severely damaged, and that can affect your speech. Actually, it's gone. Well, they'll return it to you someday, in Hell. In the meantime, your equilibrium is off. I'll make it even."

Even Shark was shocked as Justin raised his AK and obliterated Bryce's other ear.

Finn's partner lay on the deck. While he was now deaf as a

haddock, he was in no danger of dying anytime soon, which Bryce surely deemed unfortunate.

Justin walked across the deck. "Okay, assholes. You got five seconds. Who put you up to this?" As he circled his victims, he said, "Guys, so far I've just maimed you. The next shot is the exploding watermelon." Justin smirked. "Hey, you fuckos remember that old comedian? What's his name, Shark? Ya know, the guy who blew up watermelons."

Shark looked around. "I think it was Gallagher, Jus."

"Yes! *Gallagher.*" Justin checked his AK, loaded a fresh clip, and paced in more circles.

"Fun to remember that old gag." Justin rubbed his eyes. "Finn, I'm kinda runnin' outta patience. One more time. Real easy. Who put you up to hit the snare drum?"

Finn did not want to sustain another injury. "Justin, I dunno. It was all very last min—"

Blam!!

The echo of the blast saw Dogfish's head splatter across the transom.

"Tsk, tsk," said Justin. "Shark, they just don't seem to be getting it."

"All right! All fucking right! Knock it off, Justin," screamed Finn. "You just killed a good man!"

"No," responded Justin, "I just killed your X that owes us for Guild Harbor's Y. Jib Scola was a bastard, but he deserves to be vertical tonight. Sucks that you had to learn the hard way that in life, the shit that you throw at people is really a boomerang."

"Fuck," said Finn. "Fine. *Fine!* Bryce is going to have to explain the details to all of us, if he's even able to do so. Then will you leave us alone?"

"Umm . . . Odds are poor," said Justin.

CHAPTER FORTY-SIX

Kelsey's Bar, Guild Harbor

Justin noticed the creak of the door as he walked into the gin joint. He kept glancing over both shoulders, his weapon within reach. However, things felt comfortable. Quiet. The weekend was over, and the town was slowly returning to normal until the next Friday afternoon's tourist pilgrimage.

Justin surveyed the layout as he patted Michonne's shoulder.

The booths were all open except one, where Sergeant Tony O'Doul awaited his arrival.

Justin walked down the aisle toward O'Doul's booth.

"O'Doul," said Justin. "Thanks for meeting with me. Have you met my daughter?"

"No," said O'Doul. "Such a cute girl. Nice to meet you." He gently shook Michonne's hand.

"Nice to meet you too, Sergeant O'Doul," she said.

"From what I understand, Tony, you were Scola's point man. If that's true, then the time for bullshit has passed. We've had a long week," said Justin.

O'Doul nodded. He knew he'd been made. But in his portly arrogance, he still felt that there was a card to play.

"Yeah, so I heard. Some complications in dealing with Scola. Always difficult when dealing with Jib. May I speak candidly in front of your daughter?"

"Fire away, O'Doul. We just want to know what happened. Why is Scola dead, and why is my friend still at Adams-Graham over nothing? I mean *nothing*, O'Doul."

The sergeant sat back and moved his protruding stomach from one side of the booth to the other, where it finally faced magnetic north.

"There have been a lot of moving parts at play over the past week," said Justin, "but there was one piece of information that was passed along to me by the Canadians. It required a little old-school coaxing, but as usual, they rolled over like wounded sharks."

O'Doul fidgeted.

Justin continued. "Apparently, you had a major hand in scuttling a mission that was a real bitch for us. A *real* bitch, and you fucked it. Now, I understand if you want a payday, but you really tossed me, my partner, and my *daughter* into harm's way. I need answers. And that's *not* a request, O'Doul."

O'Doul had begun to sweat. He knew all about Justin McGee. He knew he was speaking to the Reaper himself. Cop or no cop, Tony enjoyed zero exemption in the eyes of Boston's most famous assassin. At that moment he felt naked, his Guild Harbor police badge worth as much as a Cub Scout camping patch.

Tony attempted to respond, but his initial words were immediately brushed away by Justin's right hand. "O'Doul. I want you to *answer* for it."

And then Justin was silent. The AC hummed and the din of the few other patrons had subsided.

"Justin," said O'Doul, "it was never personal. That Tsulio is gonna be delivered here anytime now. It didn't need to be your first voyage with the maiden stash, it could have been the next—I dunno. If we were able to clip a couple of feathers off of Scola's wings in the meantime, then why not? All's fair. I didn't tell your guys to travel hundreds of miles with nobody aboard who could vouch for the authenticity of the product. Rookie mistake, McGee. You gotta admit that some of the blame lies in the mirror."

Justin's nod was subtle. He looked at his adopted daughter, who maintained a child's peaceful demeanor, as if waiting for a turn at an arcade game.

"Michonne," said Justin, "we seem to be in the presence of

someone who put us in harm's way in order to orchestrate a way for him to make money. And in his plan, it would have been okay if we were killed. We might have had to leave Mom and our new baby alone. Honey, are you comfortable with that?"

Michonne was quiet. Her look changed as she started to stare at O'Doul with curiosity, the way one might view a frog on a dissection pad. A creature pinned with nowhere to go, and incapable of posing a threat to onlookers.

O'Doul was feeling desperate. "Look, I can arrange for the Canadians to bring the shit down. Ya know, try it again. I have that juice."

Justin scratched his head.

"How effective do you think three Canadians will be, with no legs, or ears, or maybe even heads? I actually forget how I left them. At least they had the artistic vision to repaint the deck a nice, deep maroon."

O'Doul felt the need to pee.

Justin looked at Tony. "All right, listen—we're not gettin' anywhere. Let's get outta here. Come on down the boat and let's talk like adults and figure out how we can fix everything to benefit everybody involved. I'll buy you a beer aboard my vessel."

"Okay, Justin," said O'Doul. "L-lead the way."

Justin tossed two twenties on the table and the three proceeded to walk out of the bar.

They strolled down the sidewalk in silence until Justin suggested they take a shortcut.

"Okay," said the bloated police sergeant, who sought to avoid physical exertion whenever possible.

They turned right into an alley between two multilevel buildings that would serve as a beeline straight to the *American Wake.*

They continued to walk in silence until Michonne spoke up.

"Dad, I have something that I'd like to show the police officer."

Justin nodded.

Michonne turned to Tony. "Sergeant, you wanna see something?"

O'Doul turned toward Michonne and smiled. "Sure, honey. What is it? Something from the harbor?"

Michonne looked around the alley as if innocently taking inventory of her dirty surroundings.

"No. No, sir. It's something else."

Michonne pulled a compact, sawed-off shotgun from her backpack. It was freed from its confines, cocked, and aimed at O'Doul's chest within two seconds.

"Sir," said Michonne, "I don't know who you are or exactly what you did, but my dad tells me that you put us in danger. I don't like being in danger. I *definitely* don't like seeing my dad in danger."

O'Doul couldn't believe this was real.

Michonne tilted her head, looked at him directly, and said, "I'd rather be the one who is dangerous."

Blast!

The hole that Michonne blew into O'Doul removed his entire upper body but kept the head and parts of his shoulders intact.

O'Doul died swimming in a pool of confusion and panic. His arms flapped like a butterfly for a few seconds as his nerves fired their last twitches.

Michonne calmly put the weapon away, her thoughts turning to her overdue orthodontist appointment.

CHAPTER FORTY-SEVEN

Guild Harbor Waterfront

Old tires groan and complain.

Justin watched as the bloated Cadillac Eldorado staked out some real estate in the small parking lot. The anachronistic sedan found an awkward home, straddling two corner spots.

Justin looked at the car and felt his heart rate quicken. He was still, and he instructed Michonne to do the same.

"Dad!" whispered Michonne in a harsh tone. "What is this?"

Justin stepped back, partly so he could soothe his daughter's mood with some space, but most importantly so that he could see who was getting out of the car.

"Justin McGee. Been a while. I see you have embraced some paternal instincts."

"Yeah, Darb. You know to let her be. We have our business. She has nothing to do with it."

The tall, rotund figure of Darby McBride nodded in agreement.

The Boston Irish mobster was old school, and one's family was never in danger unless they asked for it. Actually, all things considered, Darby McBride was not a danger to society anymore. These days he only caused harm to those who'd harmed him.

From what Justin could see, retirement was not treating McBride very well. He clearly had not found a new professional niche, nor had he located the health club at the senior center. "So, Jus, here we are in Guild Harbor. How do we restructure our relationship? 'Cause man, you keep finding that lucky wind gust. I can't have that in an old partner."

Justin was quiet. He looked at Michonne. He knew he couldn't just send her away to safety. This was something he had to deal with, but in a twisted way, he wanted her to learn from the exchange.

"I just want outta here, to live the rest of my life with my family. You go ahead and have a ball setting up shop, running drugs, and basically wreaking havoc on anyone you meet. I'm done, Darb. I just want to throw the lines and head offshore."

Darby McBride looked closely at Justin. "I dunno, man. You might have one last assignment in you. If you choose this piece of work, and carry it out properly, I might just look the other way while you head back to Georgia, or whatever fuckin' swamp you crawled out of."

Justin coughed. "Language, Darb, language. There's a little girl here."

Darby chuckled. "Yeah—a little girl I'm told could shoot a plum off my head from two hundred yards."

"No, that's not quite accurate. She could take out your left eye from *three* hundred deep."

A gust of wind interrupted them, and Justin looked toward the northeast. As predicted, that's where the steady breeze had planted a flag for the next twenty-four hours.

"If I carry out this assignment based on your instructions," said Justin, "then I'm assuming we're square. No more owing anybody anything. No more running. No more chasing. You can just head back to Boston."

Darby paused for a moment.

"Okay, Jus. If you do this for me, then we're square. Take your little girl, your wife, or whoever she is, and get the hell outta here. But, you gotta do this."

Justin stepped back.

"All right, Darb. What's the drill?"

"If we put our past differences aside, we might be able to assist one another with a certain *obstacle*. In the end we're both just a coupla Micks from Boston tryin' to make our way, ya know?"

"Out with it, or I'm gone, and you can spend another fortune trying to track me down."

"Okay, okay, here's the thing—even though I'm a little disappointed about our past, and I know it's an Irish thing to hold a grudge, I'm here with a proposal."

Justin looked at Michonne. "Just so you know, anything you propose has to get my daughter's approval."

Darby exploded in laughter. "What? Ha! Holy shit! You're telling me *I* need the approval of someone in a training bra to get a job done. Bullsh—"

Before Darby could finish his sentence, Michonne had rammed a Glock halfway up his right cheek.

Darby ended his clamor.

Justin exhaled and rubbed his stubble to calm the air.

"Why you're still chasing me is not a mystery, but at this point it's pretty much a waste of time. Let's move on. It sounds like there's a piece of business that you need help with. I am fortunate in that I have a solid team behind me, not least of which is this little schoolgirl here, who at a snap of my finger will end your days. How would that scuttlebutt play out at the Hibernian Club? *Notorious legend Darby McBride, taken out by a Girl Scout?*"

McBride cleared his throat.

"It's a new world, Darby. Get used to it, or cash out and go live with your sister on the Irish Riviera. Where is she, Duxbury?"

Darby was quiet, but he got the idea.

"All right, Jus. Have your girl put the gun down and I'll tell you my business. We can help each other."

Justin didn't have to say a word. He merely nodded in Michonne's direction and she brought the weapon down to her side, making it known with her resting position that it could reenter Darby's grill on command.

"Okay, here it is," said Darby calmly. "I've been looking for you, and in the process, I've cashed in some favors."

Justin was intrigued.

"I ended up crossing paths with a mutual acquaintance named Don Juan Conzalez."

Justin rolled his eyes and leaned back.

"What the hell did you get yourself into? At your age? Crazy bastard."

"I know, I know," McBride said sheepishly. "I started asking around. Anyway, I'll cut to the damn chase. This Conzalez guy—"

"Darby! This is not some *guy!* He's a Miami drug lord!"

"All right, calm down," said Darby. "I started asking questions around a few East Coast towns. Long story short, Conzalez now thinks I'm part of your crew. He associates *me* with you and your partner, Shark *Fettuccine*—whatever his name is. Shark's his real target, by the way."

Michonne interrupted. "Mr. McBride, my uncle's name is Captain Shark Bertolami."

Darby nodded in deference to the girl and continued. "Anyway, Conzalez thinks that every Mick in Boston is out to get him and is responsible for killing his niece."

"Okay, I get it. *If* I'm able to get this guy off your trail, I want an oath that you will never, ever threaten me, my family, or anyone that I have met in my life, ever again."

Darby took a gulp of the cool, salt air.

"We have a deal. Through my contacts I know that this Conzalez guy has it out big-time for your partner. To be frank, the Don knows that Shark is here and he's on his way to witness the hit personally. I have his travel information—just don't ask me what I paid to get it."

Justin looked at Michonne, who gave the wise nod of somebody thirty years her senior.

A nod is all Justin needed.

"Consider it done. If we fail in our assignment, then you still have the right to hunt me down. However, if we succeed in getting this drug lord out of your nightmares, I don't expect another threat from you for the rest of the time that anyone in my family breathes.

"Just gimme his itinerary and I'll take care of it, as long as you hold up your end of the bargain."

Darby looked at Justin. He looked at Michonne. He was finally convinced that perhaps retirement wouldn't be all that bad, especially with these allies.

"All right, Justin," said Darby. "Here's his schedule, along with his plans to find and kill Shark, and *me* while he's at it."

CHAPTER FORTY-EIGHT

Guild Harbor

It was rare for Don Juan Conzalez to ever leave Miami—although it *was* a welcome respite from Florida's oppressive early summer humidity. The Don, never fully at ease anywhere, felt especially at sea while traveling the New England coastline.

Visiting was one thing, but he never understood why anyone would choose to *live* north of Jacksonville. He found it curious why anyone would subject themselves to the relentless sting of winter when a gentler climate was a short plane ride south.

"Marco, do you have the directions to the marina where our friend, Captain Shark, is said to be docked?"

"Yeah, boss," replied the ever-loyal driver and bodyguard. "It's only about a mile up ahead."

As the Land Rover swallowed the road, a steady rain began to fall.

The Don could afford a fleet of limousines to make his travel more comfortable, but he always avoided any unwanted attention. Although he was known to be a brazen and ruthless man, Conzalez led a careful life. Those around him knew this was the key to his longevity in a business where many of his peers and competitors didn't buy green bananas.

Marco switched on the wiper blades as the steady rain made it difficult to see. He was getting too old for this line of work. He often daydreamed of one day being able to retire with the gangster's blessing and a gift of the means to relocate to Islamorada.

He loved to scour the Florida flats for bonefish while enjoying a mojito in his hand and a *chiquita* on his knee.

As the two rode in silence, Marco's eyes were trained on the wet pavement, so it was Conzalez who first noticed the young girl walking on the side of the road, obviously getting soaked.

"Marco, pull over!" yelled the Don from the backseat.

"Boss, I thought you wanted to get to the—"

"Dammit, Marco, I'm not asking permission!"

Marco rolled his eyes, pulling over on the shoulder about fifty yards ahead of the young girl.

She walked at a brisk pace, presumably to escape the rain, and within seconds she'd caught up to the idling SUV.

Conzalez rolled down the back window and motioned for her to approach the vehicle.

"Young lady," called out the Don, "it's pouring out here. Please, let me offer you a ride."

Conzalez suddenly experienced a strong sense of déjà vu which caused him to wince in pain. He remembered a similar scene on the outskirts of Havana when he'd picked up a slightly older girl who had become his adopted niece and surrogate daughter, to replace the one he'd lost so violently.

The Don's world was shattered years later when this beloved niece was murdered in cold blood by two wannabe pirates—the very ones he was about to visit, on a mission of retribution.

It had taken a substantial sum of money and many favors to finally obtain Shark Bertolami's whereabouts. Normally, the Don would have sent a hit squad to take out someone who had crossed him, but he wanted to personally savor the suffering of his niece's murderers.

While he wasn't exactly sure which of the two culprits had ended her life, in his mind they were both equally culpable and would suffer the same punishment.

The Don repeated his offer to the young girl, as she didn't seem able to hear him over the now heavier downpour.

"Dear, please come in the car and let me take you wherever you need to go. This is a nasty rain, and it's only getting worse. Come in where it's warm and dry."

The girl wiped the rain from her face.

"Sir, thank you for the offer. As you can probably imagine, my mom doesn't let me take rides from strangers. But thank you for asking.

I'm only a mile away. I'll be fine."

"Nonsense, dear. You're soaked through and sure to catch cold. Your mom has taught you well, but you must trust that I'm harmless and only want to help. I once had a little girl just like you, and a niece, God rest their souls. You're not in harm's way. Please get in—we're sort of in a hurry."

The young girl considered the offer for a few more moments.

"Okay, sir. But I'm trusting that you're not a bad man."

"No, dear. I am not a bad man," said Conzalez. "I'll take you wherever you need to go. Are you going home to your mother?"

"Yes, sir," replied the little girl. "She's expecting me. My cell phone got wet, so I can't get in touch. I'm sure she's worried sick by now."

"In that case," said the Don sincerely, "we'd better get a move on."

Conzalez opened the door and the girl crawled in.

She was panting from the brisk walk, and it took a few seconds to dry her face and hair with the handkerchief the Don handed her.

"Marco!" barked Conzalez, "there should be a blanket in the back. It's most likely buried under our gear. Find it!"

"Okay, *patron*," Marco said.

He opened the driver's door, not feeling comfortable with this situation. He thought that if the girl's mom was worried, there was a good chance she'd already notified the police. They didn't need any heat during this assignment.

Marco walked to the back of the SUV and opened the large hatch. The cargo area was stuffed with what looked like luggage and some fishing gear, which served as camouflage for the array of pistols and silencers underneath. He knew that in order to find the blanket he'd have to remove most of the trunk's contents, which meant killing precious time and getting drenched.

"Boss, you sure you—"

"Marco! Get the damned thing!" yelled Conzalez. "The poor girl is starting to shiver!"

The bodyguard/hitman began removing various contents and placing them on the wet road.

Conzalez looked at the girl. "What's your name? I'm Juan."

"My name's Michonne. Thank you very much for the ride. I'm sorry I thought that you might be a bad man. I can tell now that you're kind. I'm only about a mile away, so hopefully I won't make you and your friend late to wherever you're going."

"No worries, dear. We have all night. The start time for my meeting is rather loose. Let's get you home and we'll be on our way."

Conzalez sifted through the seat compartment and found some clean napkins which he gave to Michonne.

"You remind me of my niece. Even have a resemblance. I miss her every day."

Michonne wiped her face with the napkins. "What was her name, sir? What happened to her?"

Conzalez sighed. "Her name was Jillian. She was an angel on Earth, and now she's an angel in Heaven. Jillian and my daughter are both angels living with God. To be honest, I'm not exactly sure what happened to her. All I know is that she and my little girl are both smiling down on us this very minute."

Michonne nodded silently.

A beeping noise from the Don's phone indicated that he had just received a text message. He turned away from the girl and looked down to review the correspondence. He was alarmed, as his people knew never to interrupt his travels unless it was a matter of the utmost urgency.

He reached into his coat pocket and pulled out his reading glasses so he could read the message.

[begin ext]

Conzalez, welcome to Guild Harbor. I understand that you've come all the way from Miami to pay me a visit. I am flattered, 'cause I know you're not one to leave that greasy town unless it's due to a pressing matter. Unfortunately, I don't think our meeting will take place. You see, I also have an adopted niece. One who is even more "talented" than yours was.

See you in Hell, Juan. Save me a good seat!

Sincerely,

Captain Shark Bertolami

Conzalez's heart rate surged and his eyes bulged as he looked at the screen.

Before he could call out to Marco, Michonne extracted a Smith & Wesson from her deep coat pocket and aimed it at the Don's forehead.

She batted her eyelashes. No banter. All business. She fired. Final, and real.

The Don's head snapped back and smashed the window behind him, while his skull found air on the other side.

Michonne leapt out of the car and ran to the back where Marco stood in shock. His normally dark Cuban complexion was now an unnatural combination of alabaster and eggshell.

Marco looked at Michonne in disbelief.

"L-l-little girl, I don't know who you are or what the fuck just happened, but you and I are *both* as good as dead. Shit! What were you *thinking?* Who *are* you?"

"Sir, it's not nice to curse in the company of young girls. Didn't your mom teach you any manners?"

"Honey," said Marco, realizing this was no dream. "What are you going to do to me?"

"Well, sir, you see, I have a dilemma on my hands. I don't want to hurt you, but unfortunately you saw my face and will undoubtedly put two and two together regarding the connection between me and your targets for tonight."

Marco began to shake.

Michonne was quiet for a few seconds as she decided on her next move. In her heart, she wanted to show mercy, but unfortunately that was not an option.

"Truly, sir, I wish you were blind. I honestly do. But you're not, and that's a problem."

Michonne raised the pistol and blasted two slugs into Marco's head. He dropped to the ground immediately. Two seagulls hovered nearby. One was missing a leg.

She placed the gun in her custom-sewn deep pocket and began walking through the woods in order to get off the main road. Justin had warned her that the scene would be discovered quickly. She knew that the shortcut path would bring her behind a pizza parlor where her dad was waiting with a warm slice of pepperoni and mushroom.

CHAPTER FORTY-NINE

Office of Mayor Trish Hine

The first female mayor of Guild Harbor sat at the massive oak desk that had been used by dozens of mayors over the past two centuries. The desk was built from wood salvaged from the sailing vessel *Chrysalis* almost two hundred and fifty years ago.

The ship was a prolific supply runner that had transported munitions and hardware during the American Revolution, fortifying groups of patriots in ports all along the North Shore. The vessel left on a midnight run during the winter of 1776 but never made it out of Guild Harbor's inner waters. A gale kicked up before she could even get into open sea, and the fierce winds smashed her against the reef of rocks now known as Norman's Woe.

Fortunately, all the sailors on board survived, although several were injured, and the Americans lost a treasured vessel. The wood from the ship washed ashore and was collected by residents who wanted to preserve the vessel's memory. They brought it downtown where a volunteer master woodcrafter designed and constructed the desk where Mayor Hine now sat.

Trish Hine had always been ambitious. She resented the fact that there were still many old-timer constituents who questioned her ability to properly govern due to her gender. When she addressed the crowds at community events, she could feel the cold eyes from certain residents who would never warm up to a woman holding the mayoral gavel.

While the small city had come a long way toward freeing itself from some of the old ways of thinking, Guild Harbor still had progress to make, and Trish Hine was going to lead the way by example.

Her thoughts were interrupted by a knock at the door.

Her assistant Travis stuck his head in.

"Mayor Hine, I've got a package for you that was just delivered downstairs. There's no return address. It's a cardboard box and it's pretty light. Should I take it over to GHPD and have them give it a security screen?"

The mayor was pleased that the delivery had been made right on time.

"No, Travis. That's okay. I'm sure it's that sweater my niece said she was going to send. She borrowed it the last time she was town. Just leave it on the credenza."

"Sure thing, Mayor," said her ever-loyal assistant, who entered the room and placed the box on the antique table. Travis took a lot of flak from certain peers due to his being perceived as a bootlicker—and for a woman, no less.

Not everyone in Guild Harbor was as progressive as the majority of voters who'd put Trish in office, but fortunately for the sitting mayor, most were prepared to do it again. Many of her loyal supporters were already talking about Trish seeking the seat in the Sixth Congressional District in two years. Publicly, Trish laughed it off in a show of fake humility, but deep down she knew damn well that she was going to snatch that slot. She was tired of ribbon cuttings at hair salon openings and giving insipid speeches at Chamber of Commerce breakfasts. She belonged in Washington. In her mind, she was a star player who hadn't had a chance to take the field just yet.

The one obstacle that kept Mayor Trish Hine from organizing a campaign committee was the oldest political barrier in the world. Money.

Nobody knew that Trish and Louie were lovers, and the few that might have known—like the owner of the illicit swingers' club—were eventually disposed of.

Louie was quite handy when it came to taking out the pesky street dealers who clouded the radar screen. Trish marveled at how Louie would kill in the name of their love, and their cause.

She was still a bit surprised that Louie had legitimately fallen in love with her—that she would do anything to help her succeed and ascend. That was Louie's mistake. While Louie saw them as a couple,

Trish used her in ways the police captain could never imagine. She only wished she could actually *love* Louie, but alas, Trish was incapable of loving anyone. To the mayor, Louie was merely a pawn, like everyone else on her life's chessboard.

"If there's nothing else you need, I might head out for the day," said Travis.

"I'm all set, Travis. Have a good night," said Trish. "See you in the morning."

Her assistant shut the door behind him as he left the mayor alone with her thoughts.

Trish inhaled deeply, but calmly.

She cleared the piles of folders from her desk, each stack representing some petty local issue for which she had little to no concern.

Trish got up, walked over to the worn credenza, and brought the parcel back to the remnants of the *Chrysalis*.

She opened her top drawer and pulled out a small cutting blade which she used to slice the thick tape that was wrapped around the box.

She marveled at how light the package was, and how when you shook it there was little sound from inside.

Trish pulled apart the two cardboard sides and began sifting through layers of bubble wrap in order to find the true contents.

Peeling the plastic and tossing it on the floor, Trish finally found what she had been anticipating for several weeks.

Inside was a package stamped with an oversized maple leaf, and a yellow Post-it note that read: "Best of luck with the campaign, Congressman. Love and kisses from your friends to the north."

Trish pulled out the contents and put them on her desk.

The shipment looked so benign. So harmless.

Yet a ravenous dragon was about to be released on her unsuspecting city.

She tilted her head and smiled a cobra's grin.

Acknowledgments

There are so many people to thank that I don't know where to begin, or when I would ever stop, so to spare you, I'll keep it short.

First, I need to thank Ben Tanzer—friend, mentor, and quarterback—for his invaluable partnership during the entire *Demon Tide* project.

Many thanks to Art Vanderbilt, Eric Linder, Beth Splaine, Larry Kirwan, Peter Lucas, and Casey Sherman for their advice and encouragement, all *authors extraordinaire*.

Much gratitude to Fitzpatricks and Pollards everywhere.

I want to send out endless love and affection for my daughters, Kailee and Nicole. They humble me and make me so proud every day with their ambition and accomplishments. I hope to make them proud as well, even with this rather unorthodox vocation.

Finally, I want to take this moment to show gratitude to my dearest friend and brother, the late William S. Rizos. The separate peace that we shared was ripped away too soon, but I am eternally grateful for the times we had. *I still hear your laughter, brother.*

—**Chatham, Cape Cod**
Spring 2021

About the Author

Matt is a former investment management professional who jettisoned Wall Street to pursue his dream as a novelist. He is the proud father of two daughters and enjoys every minute of watching them thrive and excel. A licensed Coast Guard captain, Matt cherishes life by the ocean and time boating on Nantucket Sound. With a deep media background mostly steeped in radio and print, he considers it a gift to be able to tell his stories and share his life experiences through the eyes of his protagonist, Justin McGee. Matt lives on Cape Cod. For more information visit him at mattfitzpatrickbooks.com.

Also by Matt Fitzpatrick

Crosshairs and Matriarch Game

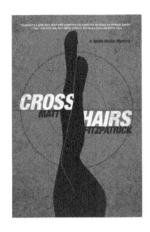

Crosshairs -
ISBN# 978-I-7320815-8-1
(Copyright 2018, Matthew S.
Fitzpatrick, Green Writer's Press)

Matriarch Game -
ISBN# 978-I-950584-50-5
Copyright 2020, Matthew S.
Fitzpatrick, Green Writer's Press)

Made in United States
North Haven, CT
29 September 2024